### "You kissed me last night."

"I know that. I was there!"

Gabe paused for a split second
"I think we should go

Bonita had been prep
cowboy, but he'd con
her, catching her off g

"You're asking me out. Perplexed,
Bonita turned her body toward the cowboy. "You
think I'm a tree-hugging elitist!"

"And you think I'm a deer-murdering hillbilly."

That made her start laughing and when she laughed
it made her headache worse. "Ow." She held her
head in her hands.

The cowboy was laughing now, too.

"For some strange reason, I do seem to enjoy
your company." She leaned her head back on the
headrest and smiled at him.

"And I enjoy yours." He glanced over at her with
those clear blue eyes that always struck a chord
somewhere deep within her. "So go out with me."

\* \* \*

**THE BRANDS OF MONTANA:**
**Wrangling their own happily-ever-afters!**

Dear Reader,

Thank you for choosing *High Country Cowgirl*, the eleventh Harlequin Special Edition book featuring the Brand family.

*High Country Cowgirl* tells the story of long-distance horse transporter and horse whisperer Gabe Brand and socialite Bonita Delafuente. Gabe Brand is a bachelor who, when he's not training million-dollar horses for high-end clients, leads a private, quiet life on a small section of Sugar Creek Ranch he's named Little Sugar Creek. When he meets Bonita, a beautiful heiress who needs her expensive show horse brought to Montana, Gabe begins to seriously rethink his bachelorhood.

Falling in love with a cowboy is not on Bonita Delafuente's mind. Instead of going on to medical school, she leaves her life in Washington, DC, to be with her mom. Her mother, who has been diagnosed with ALS, had always dreamed of retiring to a horse ranch in Montana. Finding herself in what feels like a foreign country, Bonita doesn't think much of cowboy culture— until she gets to know Gabe Brand. Gabe is kind and intelligent, and he has a gift with horses the likes of which Bonita has never seen. Just as she is losing her mom— her best friend—Bonita is finding a new home in the cowboy's arms.

I invite you to visit my website, joannasimsromance.com, and while you're there, be sure to sign up for *Rendezvous Magazine* for Brand Family Extras, news and swag. Part of the joy of writing is hearing from readers. If you write me, I will write you back! That's a promise.

Happy reading!

*Joanna*

# High Country Cowgirl

---

## Joanna Sims

HARLEQUIN® SPECIAL EDITION

Recycling programs
for this product may
not exist in your area.

ISBN-13: 978-1-335-46595-5

High Country Cowgirl

Printed in U.S.A.

www.Harlequin.com

**Joanna Sims** is proud to pen contemporary romance for Harlequin Special Edition. Joanna's series, The Brands of Montana, features hardworking characters with hometown values. You are cordially invited to join the Brands of Montana as they wrangle their own happily-ever-afters. And, as always, Joanna welcomes you to visit her at her website, joannasimsromance.com.

Dedicada a mi amiga querida...
Maria
Y a toda la ente valiente de Puerto Rico!

Dedicated to my dear friend...
Maria
And to all of the brave people of Puerto Rico!

## Chapter One

Rancher Gabe Brand would never forget the day he first saw Bonita Delafuente.

It was a typical cloudless summer day in Montana: warm enough to make a man sweat but not so hot that he couldn't get some work done at high noon. He'd finally gotten around to cleaning his two-horse trailer, something he'd been putting off for weeks. Gabe had already sweated through his shirt, so he'd taken it off and hung it on a nearby fence post. With Johnny Cash playing on the phone in his back pocket, Gabe was pouring more gas into his pressure washer when he heard the faint sound of Tater, his dog, barking from inside the house. Tater, who was geriatric at this point, preferred sleep above all activities and only made the effort to bark when someone came up the drive.

Gabe put down the gas can and walked toward the front of the house. He wasn't expecting anyone, but that didn't mean much. People often landed in his driveway hunting for the main entrance to his family's ranch, Sugar Creek.

"Hello, young man. We're looking for Gabe Brand."

An older gentleman with a full head of salt-and-pepper hair and a bit of a beer gut rounded the corner of Gabe's cabin. Walking beside the older man was a younger woman wearing English riding clothes. It was unusual to see someone wearing that kind of riding gear—most folks he knew rode Western.

"For better or worse, you found him." Gabe reached for his shirt and shrugged it on.

"I'm hoping for the better," the man said.

The minute Gabe got a good look at the woman's face, he was smitten.

"George Delafuente." The older man offered his hand. "And, this is my daughter, Bonita."

George had a firm handshake and carried himself like a man who had made his own way in the world. Gabe made note of the gold-and-diamond-encrusted Rolex his visitor was wearing. Yes, George had all of the trappings of a Montana native—jeans, cowboy boots and button-down striped shirt tucked in tight. Yet all the clothing was too clean, too new, too expensive-looking to be owned by a working rancher.

Gabe shook the man's hand and then turned his attention to the daughter.

"Beautiful," he said rather dumbly as he shook her hand.

Behind her mirrored designer sunglasses, Bonita looked at him in surprise. "I'm sorry?"

"Your name. It means beautiful in Spanish, doesn't it? That's about the only word, other than *hola* and *adios*, that I can seem to remember from high school Spanish."

Bonita pulled her hand back, her full lips unsmiling. "Yes. My parents took a gamble on that one."

No gamble at all, as far as Gabe could see. He had ranched all of his life and had made a good living training and transporting high-priced horses across the country. He'd met a lot of women along the way. None had been as lovely, to his eyes, as Bonita. Her sable-colored hair, wavy and worn loose down to her narrow waist, framed her oval face in the most lovely way; the light, occasional breeze sent tendrils of hair dusting across her tawny cheeks.

Gabe liked how slender her fingers looked as she tucked those wayward strands behind her ear. And he noted that she wasn't wearing a wedding or engagement ring on her left hand. Her handshake had been firm and strong, belying how delicate her hand seemed to be. This was a woman confident in her own skin, who seemed unafraid to assert herself in a man's world.

"Do you have a minute to talk some business?" George asked him.

Gabe caught Bonita glancing at his bare chest and stomach and fastened a couple of buttons to appear more suitable for mixed company. Everything about Bonita read class act—from her polished black riding boots to the well-tailored fawn-colored breeches that hugged her hips and shapely legs to the brilliant diamond stud earrings and matching diamond tennis bracelet.

He was sweaty and dirty and had no doubt that he'd made a less-than-sterling first impression with this woman.

"I've got a minute." Gabe gave a nod. "Can I get you folks something to drink?"

"No. Thank you." George checked his phone briefly before he continued. "We don't want to impose on you."

"No imposition." They walked together to stand in the shade of one of the large ponderosa pine trees near his cabin. "What can I do for you?"

"I'm not sure you can do anything for us, actually," Bonita said, her head turned away from him, her arms crossed in front of her body. Her body language wasn't difficult to read—she wanted to leave.

George glanced at her before he said, "We've got a horse back East that we need brought to Montana. He's a graduation present..." George smiled proudly at his daughter "...and your brother told me that you're the best transporter in the business."

"I don't know about the best, but I know what it takes to get a horse home safe." Gabe spoke to both of them, even though it seemed to him that Bonita had already made up her mind about him. "Which of my brothers has been bragging about me? My pop had a litter."

George had an easy smile; his daughter, from Gabe's brief experience, did not.

"Dr. Brand," George said. "He was out at our place for my wife's horse. Your brother is one of the most competent vets I've ever seen—and I've seen my share." The man pointed at him. "That's why I'm inclined to believe him about you."

"I've been hauling horses for the better part of my life."

Bonita had been looking everywhere but at him. "This isn't just any horse." That's when she looked at him. "Vested Interest is an Oldenburg. He's seventeen hands tall." She nodded her head toward his two-horse trailer. "That trailer is way too small."

As pretty as this woman was, Gabe bristled at the condescension in her tone. It was coming across to him that she thought he was a dumb cowboy who didn't know one horse from the next. He didn't bother to tell her that he'd trained Oldenburgs along the way—what would be the point? Yes, he could always use the business, but he wasn't going to grovel at the feet of the princess to get it.

Flatly, he said, "I don't transport long-distance in that trailer."

"You have your rig here?" George seemed to want to get the discussion back on track.

"Yes, sir."

"I'd like to see it," George said with a bit of resolve in his tone. "If that's not too much trouble."

"I've got a minute."

Gabe loved his long-distance rig and loved to show it off. And his bruised ego made him want to prove to the princess that he wasn't some ignorant yokel. It had taken him years to build his reputation; he didn't need Bonita bad-mouthing him in the high-end horse community.

"Where's the horse?"

"Northern Virginia," George told him. "Every day we board him in Virginia is another dollar we burn."

Bonita trailed behind them as they walked the short distance to an oversize garage.

"I hear that," Gabe said with a nod. "Virginia's pretty country."

"Yes, it is," George agreed. "But nothing like this land right here. This is God's country."

They reached the large garage Gabe had custom-built to house his trailer. "I can't argue with you there." He pushed the heavy door open and flipped on a light switch.

George whistled, long and appreciative. "Now, that's a fine setup!"

"Thank you," Gabe said. "She's my pride and joy."

It had taken him several years to save up enough money to put a down payment on this customized, midnight blue, luxury Equine Motorcoach. It had been his dream to own one, and it still felt a little surreal every time he took it out on the road.

George was sold—Gabe could see that. He'd earned the man's business. But he couldn't be sure of the daughter. While George set off toward the back of the long rig, Gabe was left with Bonita, who had been standing just inside of the garage in silence. He turned to face her, and that's when he saw that the lovely woman had had a slight shift in opinion of him.

Bonita slipped her sunglasses to the top of her head. The expression on her face said it all: she was impressed. Their eyes met; Gabe was immediately drawn in to rich, mahogany brown.

"This is unexpected," she told him in a blunt manner, her eyes back on the rig.

He decided not to be offended. After all, Little Sugar Creek was purposefully humble. The main house at Sugar Creek was a statement of the wealth his father had amassed, but Gabe didn't need anything fancy. He just needed comfort, function and easy-to-care-for, because he spent a good deal of his time on the road.

"All right." Bonita's body language, her tone, as well as the expression on her face, had all softened, signaling to him that she had decided to give him a chance to earn her business. "I'd like a tour."

"Hi, Mom." Bonita smiled fondly at her mother on video chat. "How are you feeling today?"

"I miss you, *mija*," her mother said, affectionately calling her "my daughter" in Spanish.

"I miss you, too, Mom. I'll be home soon."

Today was the day that Bonita had been waiting for—Vested Interest was going to begin the journey from Virginia to Montana. In advance of the trip, she had taken her father's personal private jet to Washington, DC, her old stomping grounds, and had a chance to visit with friends and go out on the town. Oh, how she missed living close to the nation's capital.

"I've got to go, Mom. Jill is driving me and we're almost there."

"Hi, Mom!" her friend Jill called out from the driver's side.

One last "I love you" to her mom and Bonita ended the video chat. With a wistful sigh, she admired the Virginia landscape. "I miss it here so much," she told her friend. Montana was picturesque, but as far as Bonita was concerned, that's all that was in the plus column. Other than that, it was desolate, backward-thinking and boring.

"We miss you!" Jill exclaimed. "Last night was long overdue."

"Agreed."

Bonita had attended graduate school at George Washington University, located in the heart of Washington, DC, and had made so many good friends along the way. Many of her friends, like Jill, went on to take jobs in Congress or went on to attend law school.

Bonita's plan had been to go to law school and then pursue a career in politics. But that was before her mother was diagnosed with an incurable, degenerative illness, amyotrophic lateral sclerosis. That devastating diagnosis changed the trajectory of Bonita's life.

Her mother, Evelyn, had dreamed of retiring to Montana. With time not on their side, her father retired early, putting the day-to-day operations of his lucrative consulting business in the hands of a chief operating officer, and bought his wife the ranch of her dreams just outside Bozeman, Montana.

Bonita, who had decided to change majors and prepared herself to attend medical school, decided to take an extended break after graduate school to help care for her mother. It hadn't been a difficult decision to make, but living in Montana had been a hard change for Bonita. She missed her cosmopolitan life—she missed her friends.

"Darn it," Jill complained. "It looks like we're here already. This visit was too short!"

"I know," Bonita agreed. She had thought she would get back to DC much more frequently than had actually happened in reality. It was difficult not to feel a pinch of envy for all of her friends who on social media seemed to be having the time of their lives. While her life seemed to have ground to a halt.

Jill pulled through the gates of Prestige Farm, a state-of-the-art equestrian facility that had been Bonita's home away from home for much of her teens and twenties. She didn't have any reason to feel nervous, and yet her stomach felt a bit unsettled. She had never had to have one of her horses transported on a trip that would take over thirty hours. Maybe that was it. Or maybe, it was the thought of encountering Gabe Brand again.

"Promise me." Jill parked her Mercedes just outside

the main office of Prestige Farm. "*Promise* me. You'll come back for another, longer visit soon."

Bonita got out, lifted her suitcase out of the trunk and shut it. "I promise."

They hugged each other tightly, sad to be parting.

"Besides, don't you want to see Mark sooner than later?"

Mark was a very handsome attorney who had been in their circle of friends for years; but this year, he was single. He had asked Bonita out for dinner her last night in DC and she had accepted, with the caveat that they were just two old friends sharing a meal. Mark had wanted to kiss her "good-night" and she had let him. It was the first kiss she had experienced since she broke things off with her college boyfriend; even a sweet kiss couldn't change how she felt about starting a new relationship. For now, her focus needed to be her mother.

"He lives here. I live there." Bonita shrugged. "I've never really liked long-distance relationships. Too much effort."

"Your father owns a private jet," Jill said, a conspiratorial gleam in her hazel eyes.

"Maybe if I met the right guy," Bonita said with another noncommittal shrug.

"Mark could be the right guy."

She didn't want to kiss and tell, so she just kept her mouth shut. But the first kiss with Mark hadn't set off any bells and whistles. Instead, she dropped the subject, gave her friend another hug and then waved as Jill drove away and headed back to her life in DC.

Luckily, Bonita didn't have a moment to be melancholy. Her longtime dressage instructor, Candace, noticed her standing in the driveway with her suitcase, looking like a waif.

"Big day!" Candace was a tall, lanky woman with cropped blond hair framing a long, tanned, makeup-free face.

"A long time coming," Bonita agreed.

They stowed her suitcase in a locker in the climate-controlled tack room and then headed toward a small turnout paddock to see her boy.

"He's been doing great." Candace leaned her arms over the fence.

Bonita felt happy, truly happy, when she was able to lay eyes on her horse again. His full name was Valdemar's Vested Interest and he had been imported from Germany two years prior as an upper-level dressage prospect. Now that she was taking a break from school, her father wanted her to get back into showing. But in her heart, Bonita wasn't sure that she wanted that for herself.

She clucked her tongue at Val to get his attention. The gelding, so regal with his long gray-and-white tail and his shiny dappled, blue-gray body, lifted his head for a brief moment before he went back to grazing. Was it right for her to take him out of the heart of dressage country and move him to cattle country?

"How have you been? How's your mother?"

Bonita filled her trainer in on the last several months of her life, trying to sound more positive about the move than she actually felt.

"Here's the million-dollar question. Have you been riding?"

They turned away from the paddock. "Honestly? Not much. I mean, I've been hopping on Mom's old girl just to keep her moving, but other than that..." Bonita's words trailed off. "I don't know what to tell you. I feel stuck since I've moved out there. Frozen. I feel completely out of my element, disoriented. I just can't seem to get myself motivated to do much of anything, other than making sure Mom's okay. I'm hoping Val will give me the motivation I need to snap out of it."

"I'll tell you what," Candace said, "Once you get Val settled, I'll come out to Montana. He's fit. He's been on a strict training program. He's not the kind of horse you can leave to his own devices. You've got to get him back into his workout routine immediately."

"I will. I promise. And yes to you coming for a visit."

Candace got a text on her phone. "Your transporter is being buzzed in at the gate right now."

There it was—that flip-flop in her stomach at the thought of seeing Gabe again.

Even after Gabe showed her his rig, even after she had checked his credentials, followed up with references, checked prices to fly Val to Montana, interviewed other cross-country transport companies, Bonita kept coming back to Gabe Brand.

She had been impressed with his rig—it was top-notch, with all the safety features and comfort necessary for such an extensive trip. Gabe had contacts with quality stables along the route so they could stop and let Val rest overnight. The rig was also equipped with a box stall so that Val could move around and stretch his neck down, which would lessen the risk of respiratory problems from the trip.

Even though she had dismissed him in the beginning, after speaking with Gabe about his transport experience and probing his knowledge about horses, Bonita couldn't dismiss him for long.

Gabe Brand pulled up to the secured gate of Prestige Farm after traveling for several days. He had been able to coordinate a delivery of a quarter horse to a facility in Maryland before heading down to Virginia to pick up the Oldenburg.

He loved being on the road, just him and his dog, Tater. The peace and quiet of the road was something he craved during the spells when he didn't have any transport business on the books.

"Gabe Brand," he spoke into the intercom. "I'm here to pick up Vested Interest."

The ornate gate, decorated with intricate scrollwork and a large gold horseshoe in the center, slowly opened. Gabe had been to a lot of barns, big and small, but this was one of the swankier facilities he'd ever visited. The place just said "money." The barn didn't even resemble a barn—it looked more like a fancy stucco hotel with brick pavers leading up to a two-story clubhouse.

"Fancy." Gabe found a place to park his rig near what appeared to be the main entrance of the barn.

The rancher grabbed his cowboy hat and gave Tater, who was curled up in the front seat, a quick pat on the head. "I'll let you out on the grass before we take off," he promised his tiny canine companion.

Gabe hopped out of the truck, shut the door and turned to head to the front office.

"Hi."

"Holy Jesus, woman! You scared the living daylights out of me."

Bonita, a person he didn't expect to see, had sneaked

up on him out of nowhere. She was just as pretty on second look as she had been on the first; her hair was braided into a thick, single plait and she was wearing slim-fit jeans that hugged her body in the right ways. Her face was made-up, just like the first day they had met, and it made him wonder what Bonita looked like without a full face of makeup.

"All I did was say hi," she countered.

"I suppose I didn't expect to see you here today." Gabe tipped his hat to her. "How do?"

"I'm doing okay. A little anxious. Val's paperwork is in order, he's up-to-date on all of his shots and he's been given a clean bill of health. One of the stablehands is putting on his shipping boots right now."

Gabe nodded. She had just answered most of the questions he was going to ask any warm body he could find at the front office.

"Any loading issues with this horse?"

"No." She gave a little shake of her head. "And my trainer said he's always been a good traveler, so we shouldn't have any problems along the way."

Gabe stopped in his tracks. "Hold up. What do you mean by 'we' exactly?"

"Oh." Bonita looked him straight in the eye, her jaw setting. "Didn't I tell you? I've decided to tag along."

## Chapter Two

"Here's the health certificate with a current Coggins test." Candace handed Gabe the paperwork. "I think you're all set. You've got enough of his food and hay to last you until you get him home, paperwork—"

"Horse," Bonita filled in for her trainer with a smile.

"Most important." The trainer opened her arms for a hug.

It had taken twenty minutes to get Val loaded into the rig. It was the first time Candace had ever had issues loading the show horse, and Bonita hoped it wasn't an omen of things to come.

"We're all going to miss you here." Candace stepped back after they hugged tightly. "But as soon as you're ready for me, I'll come to you."

"Ready?" Gabe had left them for a moment but returned much too quickly. Saying goodbye to Candace meant closing a chapter of a life she had loved dearly.

Bonita nodded, blinking hard several times to stop tears from welling in her eyes. She leaned down to pick up her small suitcase, but Gabe beat her to it. With her suitcase in one hand, the cowboy opened up the side door to his rig, a door that led into the living area, and nodded for her to go up the small flight of stairs.

"I'll just put your bag right here for now." Gabe tucked her suitcase into one of the cabinets that lined the wall.

Her arms crossed in front of her body, Bonita said, "That's fine."

Her plan was unfolding perfectly, and yet she hadn't accurately imagined what it would *feel* like to be alone with Gabe, a virtual stranger. It felt, as it turned out, awkward and odd.

"You're welcome to ride back here," Gabe said, his body stiff. She guessed that he was feeling as uncomfortable as she was by her decision to hijack the trip. "Catch you a nap if you want."

"I have to ride up front," she explained. "Car sickness."

She didn't imagine it—he looked pretty disappointed by that bit of news.

"Well," Gabe said slowly. "Tater usually rides up front with me."

Tater, having heard her name, gave one, high-pitched bark.

So Bonita wasn't the only passenger. A lover of all animals, her awkwardness temporarily forgotten, Bonita walked past the cowboy to the front of the rig. The moment she saw the little dog, she felt happy. She wasn't alone with Gabe—they had Tater!

"You have a Chihuahua?"

"That's Tater," he said. "Be careful. She's old and she can get snappy every now and again."

Bonita ignored the warning and scooped up the little dog into her arms. "Please," she said to him. "We are both Mexican Americans. We are destined to get on." To

Tater, she asked, *"Tu hablas español, mi perrita?"* Bonita smiled at Gabe. "I asked her if she speaks Spanish."

He adjusted his cowboy hat to sit a bit farther back on his head. She could see his eyes better, and she was struck by how clear and bright those eyes really were.

"She knows *uno, dos* and *tres*. I didn't teach her four, on account of the leg."

For the first time that day, Bonita truly felt like laughing. So the cowboy had a sense of humor. That could make the trip a little more interesting. "That was probably the right thing to do," Bonita agreed. "What happened to your leg, little one?"

"That's just how God made her."

"Well—she's perfect."

Tater had managed to break the ice between the cowboy and her. Bonita took her place in the passenger seat, buckled up and then put the dog in her lap.

Gabe got himself situated behind the wheel of the large rig and cranked the engine. On the dashboard, a screen turned on and a live video feed of her horse appeared.

"This way, we've got eyes on him the whole trip," Gabe said. "We'll be stopping in Columbus, Ohio, for the night…give his legs a rest."

Bonita watched the horse on the screen, still in awe that he was actually hers, as they slowly made their way to the gate. As the gate swung open, she looked at the equestrian complex she had called home in the side view mirror, feeling nostalgic for another time, when her mom was healthy and she was under the illusion that nothing in her life could go wrong. That's how it had been while she was riding here. It had been an idyllic life and it was over. Now she knew that plenty could go wrong. In fact, her whole world could shatter with one diagnosis.

"I hope you like music." Gabe switched on the radio.

She did like music. All kinds. Reggae, classic rock, salsa, jazz—she liked virtually all genres of music. The one kind of music she couldn't stand? Country. What did Gabe play for the entire seven hours it took to get to their first stop? Country.

Bonita tried several different strategies to cope with the onslaught of her most hated genre of music: listening to her own music with her earbuds, striking up a conversation with the cowboy, counting telephone poles, scrolling through her social media, texting friends and mindful meditation. She even contemplated braving a bout of motion sickness by escaping to the back, but the thought of losing her lunch in Gabe's super expensive Equine Motorcoach made her think better of it. Instead, she sat in stoic silence, internally cursing all country singers and over-petting poor Tater's head. The only reprieve she got was when they had to stop for fuel and a bathroom break for the Chihuahua.

"Do you need anything?" she asked before heading into the convenience store.

"No. I'm good. Once I'm done filling up, I'm gonna check on Val before we take off again."

Bonita dawdled in the convenience store. She knew Gabe was probably ready to roll and she just couldn't quite bring herself to hurry. She had physically shaken her head in the bathroom in an unsuccessful attempt to get Blake Shelton out of it. By the time she left the store with her soda, something she promised she wouldn't drink on the trip, and a candy bar, something she promised herself she wouldn't eat on the trip, Gabe had the rig parked near the exit. He was definitely waiting on her.

"How is he?" she asked as she climbed into the rig, juggling her drink and candy bar.

"Good."

He was annoyed.

"Buckle up." He already had the engine cranked. "We're on a schedule."

She took Tater from him, settled the dog on her lap and then she did buckle up, but she did it rather slowly. He might be annoyed with her, but she was the one who had to marinate in Johnny Cash for heaven only knew how much longer.

"How much longer do we have?" she asked over the music.

"Just shy of an hour."

*¡Ay Dios mio! ¡Por favor, no mas musica!*

She prayed to God to make the music stop. Her prayers were not answered and ol' Johnny kept on singin'. She had thought several times to ask him to turn the music off for a bit, yet she was acutely aware of the fact that she was the one crashing this party. She hadn't trusted him with nearly a million dollars of her father's money—that was the truth. But crashing the party *and* making demands was even a step too far for her.

"I've never been to Ohio," she said, more to herself than to Gabe. For miles and miles, the terrain had been flat, and cows occupied the fields more often than not. Ohio seemed to be as rural and lonely in places as Montana, minus the mountains. Even though she didn't like the fact that rush hour traffic was slowing them down in Columbus, she was glad to see civilization. She liked to see people—she liked the energy of a big city.

"What's that?" Gabe switched off the radio.

*Gracias a Dios.* Bonita silently thanked God.

"I've never been here." She gestured out the windshield. "Ohio."

Gabe nodded wordlessly.

"Where are we stopping for the night?"

"My friend's got a spread not too far from here. Plenty of room for Val to let loose some energy. Doc's ready for him—got a stall set up for tonight."

She assumed that Doc was the friend; she didn't ask because she was tired and feeling irritable. She'd find out soon enough one way or the other.

"I don't know how you do this all the time," Bonita muttered and shifted uncomfortably in her seat. The drive was tedious, just one endless mile after another. "Don't you get tired of it?"

"Sometimes," Gabe said. "But this is part of how I make a living, so I get over it quick enough."

He thankfully took the next exit and then they went deep into the back roads on the far outskirts of Columbus. There were more miles with more cows and more dilapidated barns in more flat fields, and then Bonita spotted the sign announcing that they had finally arrived at their destination: Hobby Horse Farm.

It was a lovely farm. The crown jewel was a whitewashed Victorian farmhouse with a wraparound porch, carved gables and two stately brick chimneys. There were miles of green pastureland, white fences and grazing horses dotting the landscape. She hugged Tater to her body a little too hard in her excitement, and the dog gave a grunt of discomfort.

"Oh! I'm sorry, little one." She kissed the dog on the head. "I'm just so happy that we're finally here!"

"Gabe Brand, as I live and breathe!"

*Doc* turned out to be a wiry woman, possibly in her late forties. She had a wild mass of copper curls and deep smile lines around her eyes and mouth. She was dressed in riding boots and breeches and she was waving her arms in the air in enthusiastic greeting. A small pack of dogs—old, young, small and large— surrounded Gabe's friend, barking and tails wagging. Not to be outdone, Tater began to alternate between growls and woofs.

Gabe stuck his hand out the window and waved. "Where do you want her?"

"Pull straight on in." The woman pointed to the large gravel area ahead. "It'll hold you."

He parked and hopped out of the rig. Bonita was glad to follow. Carrying Tater, she rounded the front of the rig and caught the greeting between friends. The woman, who seemed to jerk from one position to the next in big leaps and movements, tossed her arms over Gabe's shoulders and kissed him right on the lips. It wasn't a lingering kiss, but Bonita sure didn't recall greeting any of her friends—male or female—with a kiss on the lips.

"Goodness gracious, I'm glad to see you." Doc exclaimed, her hands now on her boyish hips. "It's been too long."

Like a bee in search of nectar, their hostess flitted toward her, a wide, welcoming smile on her face. The woman invaded her personal space and stuck out her hand. "Janice Joplin. Same sound, different spelling.

I know, can you believe it? I married into the name. I thought about changing it after the divorce, but by then I'd been Doc Joplin for years, so why bother. I can't sing, I've never had a drug problem, I'm not kin. So there you go."

It took Bonita a split second to realize that Janice had finished, come up for air and was waiting on her now.

"Bonny." She told Janice her nickname, sometimes a little shy about her own given name, while Janice's pack of dogs wove around her legs, smacking her legs with their wagging tails. Tater was snarling at the circling, friendly pack of canines, showing her teeth and growling low in her throat.

"She's the owner," Gabe told Janice, and Bonita got the impression that he wanted to quickly clear up any confusion regarding her status.

"Perfect. Nice to meet you," Janice said before she lurched away, her attention now on the horse in the rig. "Let's see what you've brought me!"

Gabe grabbed the health certificate that had allowed them to travel across state lines with Val and handed it to Janice. Their hostess scanned the document, nodded quickly and handed it back.

"Doc is one of the few large animal veterinarians who specialize in acupuncture," Gabe told Bonita as they walked to the back of the rig. "My brother Liam worked with her right out of vet school."

Hands on her hips, Janice had moved on from small talk and her focus was on Val. "Let's get him out of there and into the pasture."

Gabe lowered the hydraulic ramp and hooked a lead rope to Val's halter. Wide-eyed, ears forward, head bobbing up and down, Val was anxiously pawing at the ground, wanting to be free from his mobile stall.

Janice whistled her appreciation. "I do love an Oldenburg. You've got a nice horse here."

Val came down the ramp, his nostrils flared, snorting loudly at the nearby horses. It was strange—Val was Bonita's dream horse, and yet there was something that made her feel cautious around him. The horse was giant, muscular and in peak fitness. When his head was raised and he was wild-eyed and anxious, he was a handful.

Gabe, calm in the face of the horse's natural fear and anxiety, handed the lead rope to Janice. He bent down and started to remove Val's padded shipping boots from each leg, staying with the horse no matter how rambunctious he got.

"I know," Janice said in a soothing voice to the nervous horse, rubbing his neck. "It's all so strange."

Glad to have the excuse of holding Tater, Bonita stood back, letting the other two handle Val. She had always felt a connection to every horse she had ever owned. But this time, she only felt nervous around Val. No connection. And it worried her. Her father and mother, who wanted her to continue showing, had picked out Val for her, and who would say no to a dream horse as a graduation present? It was the first time she hadn't picked out her own show horse. Standing in Ohio, not wanting to engage with her new horse, made Bonita think that she should have said no.

"Where do you want him?" Gabe asked, taking the lead rope again.

"Take him to this pasture right here." Janice pointed to an unoccupied pasture to her left. To Bonita, she added, "He'll have the whole place to himself, so you won't have to worry about him getting injured."

Horses were herd animals, and as prey animals, they were highly alert to any possible danger. They were always curious about any new horse that appeared on the scene and the Oldenburg's arrival was no exception. As Val pranced alongside Gabe, tossing his head and letting his tail fly like an unfurled flag behind him, all of the horses on the property had come to the edge of their fences and were watching attentively. Some of them started to run in their pastures, snorting and bucking and kicking at their pasture-mates. Others followed Val on their side of the fence, trying to catch his scent.

The moment Val was let off his lead, the Oldenburg exploded, bucking several times, farting and kicking out his hind legs, before he galloped to the far end of the pasture.

"He's got a run-in shed, water, plenty of grass to eat. We can feed him with the others in about an hour or so, but that's up to you," Janice said.

"That's fine." Bonita gave a little shrug.

Val was touching noses across the fence with one of Janice's horses. After a moment, both horses squealed and kicked at each other. Janice's horse moved, which meant that Val won the higher spot in the hierarchy.

"He's fine," their hostess announced. "Let me show you the barn."

"I'm going to clean out the rig real quick." Gabe split off and walked away.

"You can dump your manure on the compost pile out back."

"I think I'd better let Tater down for a moment," Bonita said. "Do you think she'll be okay with all of your four-legged friends?"

"Tater can handle her own." Janice laughed. "She'll be running this pack in five seconds flat, just you watch. Besides—they know each other. A couple of sniffs here, a couple of sniffs there, and they'll be all reacquainted."

Bonita was still reticent about putting Tater down but just as Janice had predicted, the three-legged Chihuahua wasn't a pushover. Even so, after Tater finished her business, Bonita scooped her back up and tucked the dog into the crook of her arm.

"I appreciate you letting us rest here for the night." Bonita had to work to keep stride with Janice, who walked as fast as she talked.

"Oh. No problem," her hostess said in a breezy manner. "Gabe's been stopping here for years. We're always tickled to see him."

Bonita followed Janice to the backside of the two-story Victorian, only to realize that the barn was actually attached to the house.

"This is amazing!" Bonita exclaimed, her eyes wide. "I have always wanted to have my house attached to my barn."

Janice opened a small white picket gate that led into the stable. "I love it. But it's an albatross. I'll be hard-pressed to ever sell it, that's a fact. Not many people want to live with their horses."

"I would."

"I like you already," Janice said before she stopped in front of an empty stall. "Val will bed down in here tonight."

"Okay." Bonita was looking everywhere, trying to take it all in at once. "This place is too cool."

"It was built back in the days when people wanted the heat from the animals to help heat the house," Janice said. "It burned down once and got rebuilt sometime in the early 1900s. I can't tell you how convenient it is during the winter or if one of mine is sick. I just come out here in my slippers and my nightgown. Done and done."

Bonita thought they were still walking forward when Janice circled back, into her personal space again, and stopped. "So you and Gabe aren't together?"

"No." It struck Bonita as strange that anyone would put Gabe and her together as a couple; they were so different. "I kind of crashed the trip."

"I knew it had to be something. Gabe doesn't let clients travel with him. Some have followed behind him but never with him. Well." Janice gave a disappointed cluck of her tongue. "That's too bad. It'd be nice to see him settled down after all this time. I'm afraid he's getting cemented in his ways and becoming an incorrigible bachelor. Not that I have room to talk, mind you. I'm divorced, my kids are grown, and other than fixing the fences, what do I need a man for?"

Janice opened a door that led into the farmhouse. "I just opened a bottle of red."

A glass of wine, or two, was *exactly* what Bonita needed after seven straight hours of country music. She followed Janice from one part of her world, the barn, into the other part of her world, the farmhouse, which was infused with the scent of beef stew and greens simmering on the stove. The decor was eclectic and a bit eccentric and it was a total reflection of Janice's free-spirited personality. Everything in the house seemed to be collected from various yard sales, thrift stores and side-of-the-road antique marts. Nothing matched—the chairs around the kitchen table were mismatched, the fabrics on the couch and chairs in the living room where mismatched, and the dishes were all mismatched. And yet everything blended together, much like a tapestry, into one wonderfully homey picture.

"I didn't know to expect you." Janice handed her a glass of wine.

"I'm so sorry," Bonita apologized. "I just assumed Gabe let you know."

"He might've thought he did and then it slipped his mind. He's like that. Don't worry. I'm just thinking out loud… I have a spare room. You'd be more comfortable in here than out there in the rig, don't you think?"

Actually…

"You wouldn't mind?"

Janice waved her hand and frowned at her as if she thought the question was the most ridiculous thing she had ever heard. She went to the front door, pulled it open, stood on the front porch and hollered to Gabe.

"Gabe! Bring Bonny's suitcase in here when you're done! She's bunking with me tonight!"

"I can go get it." Bonita put her glass down on the butcher-block island in the kitchen. Asking Gabe to wait on her like a bellboy was only adding insult to his injury. He hadn't wanted her on the trip in the first place.

"He can get it." Janice shooed her back into the kitchen. "You hang out here with me and keep me company. I'm surrounded by horses, cows, manure and men. I don't get nearly enough estrogen in my life, *that* I can tell you!"

## Chapter Three

After dinner, Gabe found Bonita in the barn, sitting on a tack box across from Val's stall, holding another glass of wine in her hand. When she saw him, she scooted over and made room for him to sit down beside her.

"They're a loud bunch," Gabe said as he sat down next to his client, careful to make sure that there was plenty of space between Bonita's body and his.

She had been staring at her horse, swirling her wine around and around in the glass. She seemed lost in her own thoughts and from the look on her face—a sincerely pretty and compelling face—they weren't the happiest thoughts in the world.

"They are wonderful." Bonita's full mouth turned up in a slight smile. "Truly. Stopping here was a real blessing."

"Good." Gabe was glad to hear it. Even though he hadn't wanted her along for the trip, he had an instinct to make sure she was safe and cared for while she was with him. Not that he had anything in particular against Bonita—he just preferred to travel alone. It was his policy and that way he could say no to anyone and everyone who asked. And clients did ask. Bonita was the only client who wouldn't take no for an answer. And he'd adapted. That was his way. He hadn't liked it, but he dealt with it.

His mother died when he was just a kid and his father, Jock, told him straight up that he'd better learn to deal with life's curveballs quick, because they came fast and furious sometimes. It was one of his father's better pieces of advice and Gabe had been adapting to change quickly ever since.

Bonita took a small sip of her wine. She seemed a little more relaxed and if he had counted correctly, she was on her third glass. She said, "Janice is crazy. I *love* that about her."

Looking straight ahead, Gabe nodded with a little smile. "She's a nut, that's the truth."

"You've known her a long time."

It was more of a statement than a question.

"A long time."

His companion took another sip of the wine before she said, "The way she is with her ex, you'd think they were still a couple."

Janice had invited her ex-husband, Gary, for dinner, along with a group of friends, all from the same horse community that Gabe hadn't seen in a long time. Gary was a solid horse trainer in his own right and Janice still regularly referred her clients to him if they had a horse with training concerns.

"They're much better friends than spouses."

"That's rare."

He nodded. He'd never managed to stay friends with his exes. For him, once it was over, it was time to move on. It had been quite a while since he'd had to move on from a woman, though. He'd managed to fill his life with his horses. The last time he had to move on had broken his heart good and proper.

"I love the barn at night," Bonita mused quietly. "Don't you?"

He glanced at Bonita's profile. It was his favorite time in the barn. In that moment, Gabe realized that he was enjoying sitting in the barn with Bonita a little too much. Instead of answering, he stood up.

"I'm going to turn in. We've got a long stretch tomorrow. I want to leave by four."

His client's sleepy eyes opened wide as she looked up at him. "In the morning?"

He nodded.

"That means I have to get up at three?"

"If it takes you an hour to get ready, then I suppose so."

Bonita frowned.

"I want to get to our next stop by late afternoon. That'll give Val plenty of time to stretch out his legs."

Still frowning, Bonita asked, "Where's our next destination?"

"I have Val booked for a stall in a facility in Grimes, Iowa."

"Iowa," she repeated so morosely that it made him smile. "How many hours to *Grimes*?"

"Ten," he told her. "Today was a short day."

"It didn't feel short."

"It was."

They stared at each other for a second or two before Gabe broke the eye contact and waved his hand. "I'll see you in the morning."

"Hey…"

He turned back to her.

"Do you mind if I keep Tater with me tonight?"

He couldn't believe how long it took him to process that question. He was just used to having Tater with him.

"Sure," he finally said. "If it'll make the night better for you."

"Gracias." Bonita said, the word of thanks rolling off her tongue in a way that sounded mighty pleasant to his ears.

"De nada." His *you're welcome* came out stilted and heavily accented, but it made her smile, and he liked to see that smile.

With one final nod to his client, he left the barn and headed out to the rig. He planned on taking a quick shower, climbing into the sleeping bunk above the front cab and getting at least eight hours of shut-eye. He was lucky that he could fall asleep on a dime, and now that he didn't have to worry about walking around the rig in his boxers, he could get comfortable and get down to the business of sleeping.

Morning came too early for Bonita. Soon after Gabe gave her the bad news about her three o'clock wake-up time, she finished her wine, made sure Tater had one last visit to a grassy spot on the lawn, said good-night to her new friends and then retreated to the guest room. After a long, hot shower and going through her nightly routine of brushing her teeth and putting on her face creams and brushing all the tangles out of her waist-length hair, as she always did, she called her parents to say good-night.

"I have to get up at three o'clock in the morning," Bonita complained to her father. No matter how far into adulthood she got, she still went to her dad for comfort when life seemed unfair.

"*And* I'll be subjected to another ten hours of country music, which feels like a form of torture."

"I don't even know why you insisted on going," her father said. "I told you I trusted the man."

"I know," she acknowledged. "I didn't."

"How about now? You've spent the day with him. What's the verdict?"

Bonita knew exactly what her father was driving at. He wanted her to admit that she was wrong.

"He seems competent," she admitted, not saying the words *you were right, I was wrong*.

"Then come home now," George suggested. "You're right there near Columbus. I'll send my pilot to come pick you up. There's an executive airport there—I've used it before. If you're not happy, come home."

Yes, she didn't want to get up at three o'clock in the morning. Who did? And, yes, she dreaded the hours of monotonous highway and basting in the music of every country artist known to mankind, but it hadn't occurred to her—not once—to throw in the towel.

"I'm not unhappy."

"You could have fooled me, *mi corazón*."

Did she want to take her father's offer and bail on the trip? Gabe was more than competent. He knew how to handle horses, that was easy to assess after a day. The way he handled a flighty, excitable horse like Val had been impressive.

"I'm just talking." She backpedaled a bit. "Val is my horse. I'm responsible for him now. I'm going to stick it out. This is far from the worst experience I've ever had to go through."

After those words, they both were silent and Bonita knew exactly what her father was thinking: her mother's illness was the worst thing either one of them had ever gone through and the worst was yet to come.

"Is Mom awake?" Bonita was the first to break the silence. "I'd like to say good-night."

"She asked the nurse to put her to bed early tonight."

Bonita had been lying back on a stack of pillows, but she sat up instinctively. "Is she okay? Do I need to come home now for her?"

"She's fine," George said and for the first time Bonita heard weariness in her father's voice. "It's been a bad day... She has those. Tomorrow will be better. If you want to stay with Val, your mom will be fine until you return."

After she hung up the phone with her dad, Bonita spent some time catching up with friends on social media. She sent a friend request to Janice—they had struck up a friendship in a short time and they both wanted to keep in touch—and then she shut off the light.

Bonita had been an insomniac for years. Even with the three glasses of wine, she was wide-awake listening to the sounds drifting up the hallway from the kitchen, staring at the ceiling.

It felt as if her life had taken some odd turns of late. She was in a farmhouse in Ohio, getting ready to head off to Iowa with a cowboy she didn't know all that well, instead of starting her first year of medical school. Her mother's illness was a major driving force for her eventual return to the pursuit of a medical degree. She wanted to be able to help other families whose lives had been turned upside down, much as hers had, by a single diagnosis. Bonita didn't regret putting her dream on hold to spend time with her mother in her final years. Her only regret was that she hadn't come home sooner.

Gabe was already in the barn with Val when Bonita shuffled into the barn, blurry-eyed and running on only two hours of restless sleep, carrying Tater in one hand and rolling her suitcase behind her with the other.

"He's been fed." The cowboy seemed to forget to engage in the social routine of greeting each other before getting down to business.

"Good morning to you, too," she said grumpily.

Gabe glanced at her before he kept on shoveling the manure out of Val's stall. "If you want to grab his shipping boots, I'll get him ready to load."

Bonita checked to make sure the gates between the barn and the outside were closed before she put Tater down. She gathered up the tall, padded shipping boots and carried them over to Gabe.

"Hi there, Val." She reached out and let the horse smell her hand. "How's he doing?"

"He's being a horse." Gabe knelt down by Val's hind leg and secured the shipping boot.

Val was throwing his head, backing up to avoid Gabe and acting like he was going to bite her.

"Hey." Bonita pushed the horse's mouth away with her hand. "He's a lot more mouthy than I remember."

Gabe finished his job and stood up. "He's got a few bad habits."

He looked fresh and crisp. He was wearing his usual button-down shirt, tucked in tightly, straight-leg denim jeans, cowboy boots, a cowboy hat and a leather belt with an oval silver buckle. It was indecent to look that put-together and awake in the middle of the night. In contrast, she had barely managed to get her hair into a ponytail, and she was wearing a baggy sweatshirt and jeans with no makeup. Her eyes were puffy, her face felt puffy—she needed coffee and some sort of food to help settle it.

"I don't suppose breakfast is in our future?"

"I doubt we're going to find anything open for a while. I've got some rations in the kitchen. You can help yourself."

Gabe was ready to go. She stepped out of the way so he could lead Val out of the stall. She quickly scooped up Tater and followed behind with her suitcase. Again, it took Gabe several tries to get him in the trailer.

"I don't know what's wrong with him. Candace swears he's never had any loading issues."

Gabe shut the back of the rig and secured it. "He's got them now."

There it was again, that little gnawing sensation in her stomach about her new horse. He was such a beautiful creature; maybe it was just going to take some time for them to bond.

"Goodbye, Hobby Horse Farm," Bonita said as they slowly pulled out onto the desolate road. It was so dark that it didn't feel like morning to her at all. "I'm sorry I didn't get to say one more goodbye to Janice."

"She's not a morning person."

"That makes two of us."

"I love this time of day. No people. No traffic. It's the best time to travel."

Deciding not to argue with an obvious morning person, Bonita took Gabe up on his offer and found some breakfast bars in the kitchen. She also discovered that

Gabe had made a pot of coffee and it was still warm enough to tolerate.

Tater found her bowls of food and water while Bonita searched for some creamer for her coffee.

"Do you have any creamer?"

"I drink it black."

"Shoot." So much for coffee.

With a bottle of water and a breakfast bar in hand, Bonita slumped into the passenger seat.

"You know, my father wanted me to fly home from Columbus. There's creamer on the jet."

"Hard to keep an eye on me from the sky." Gabe didn't crack a smile, but she believed that he meant for there to be humor laced with truth in that statement.

"I'm not keeping an eye on you," Bonita retorted quickly. Then, she revised her answer a bit a second later. "I *was* keeping an eye on you."

"That seat leans back," Gabe told her. "Why don't you shut your eyes and try to get some more sleep? I promise I won't screw anything up until after you wake up."

She didn't know if he was trying to avoid her grumpiness or was sincerely concerned for her well-being, but it didn't matter. It was a good idea and she took him up on it. She finished her breakfast bar and water, then leaned back and closed her eyes. It seemed that Gabe didn't listen to music early in the morning, and that suited her just fine. She felt herself drifting to sleep but was awakened by Tater yipping next to her. Not opening her eyes, she reached down, felt for the little dog and lifted her onto her lap.

"Go to sleep," she mumbled. Those were the last words she wanted to utter until the sun rose and it was officially morning.

* * *

Gabe drove for hours without his usual music in the background. Bonita had fallen asleep quickly and he didn't want to disturb her.

It wasn't ideal that he had someone else to consider on this trip. He had his routine, his way of doing things to make the trips easier, but he also found some upsides to having a passenger. Even though they hadn't passed the time talking, just having Bonita's presence had made the trip go a bit faster for him. And she smelled nice—like lavender. In fact, the last thought he had before he fell asleep was how sweet Bonita smelled when he was sitting so close to her on that tack box.

She didn't snore, but she mumbled several times in her sleep. He couldn't make out the words, but he found himself wondering about Bonita Delafuente.

She wasn't quite as one-dimensional as he had judged after their first meeting. Yes, she was entitled, as most people from wealthy families were, but she wasn't a snob. The way she took to Janice and Hobby Horse Farm, the kindness she had shown to all of his friends, made him realize that he had labeled her too harshly. Bonita held herself a bit stiff, and her appearance was polished—her nails perfectly done and her expensive jewelry was part of the uniform—but she had a million-dollar smile and a laugh that made a man want to listen for a long time. And she was smart. That he especially liked. It wasn't too often that he saw a woman go toe-to-toe intellectually with Janice, but Bonita did. Easily.

His client stirred in the passenger seat, making sounds that let him know she was waking up from her nap. Yawning long and loud, Bonita opened her eyes.

"What time is it?"

"Just after nine."

Tater, who had jumped down from Bonita's lap some time ago, heard her voice and raced up to the front from the back of the rig.

Sitting up, Bonita reached down to pet Tater. "I've been asleep for five hours?"

"Just about."

She stretched her arms, groaned and then yawned again. "Coffee."

That one word made Gabe smile. He didn't know why he found Bonita's grouchiness adorable instead of annoying.

"I'll pull off at the next exit. Tater needs a break and we could use some gas."

"How's Val?"

"Eating hay."

Out of habit, Gabe glanced at the screen to his right showing a live video stream of Val. If he was eating hay and making manure, most likely all was well with the Oldenburg.

Gabe had a feeling from his first meeting with Bonita that she had him written off as a dumb cowboy. It wouldn't be the first time in his life that high-end horse owners had prejudged him. But his ability with horses spoke for itself and people who wrongly judged him usually paid a premium to hire him again. He'd seen a small shift in Bonita; yes, she was a skeptic or she wouldn't have insisted on babysitting him on a road trip, but he felt her trust in him growing. And for whatever reason, in particular, he wanted Bonita to trust in him.

"Can I get anything for you?" Bonita asked after another yawn and stretch.

"No. I'm good."

He had stopped to fill up the tank with fuel and give his passenger and Tater a break from the road. Bonita wasn't used to road trips; she was used to taking a quick flight to her destinations on her father's private jet. Traveling on the road could be tedious, he more than anyone knew that, and they would just be reaching the halfway mark when they would pull in to Grimes later on today.

As he watched Bonita walk toward the convenience store, her oversize sweatshirt swallowing the top half of her body and her long, ponytail swinging behind her, he was actually shocked that she hadn't jumped at the chance to fly back to Bozeman. His first thought was that she didn't trust him to get Val home safely, but then he reconsidered. Bonita appeared to be the type of woman who didn't like to fail at anything. Perhaps leaving a challenging trip early would have been a sign of defeat to her. If he was right, he could respect that about her.

He was just wrapping up his business at the pump when Bonita rejoined him, carrying two fountain drinks and a bag full of donuts.

"I got some for you, too," she said, unhappily.

"Thank you." He didn't indulge in sugar too much with the hours of sitting he had to do when he was transporting. But he wasn't going to turn down a nice gesture on her part.

Still frowning, Bonita looked at her purchases. "Just look what this trip has done to me already. I'm in sweats, I haven't brushed my hair, no makeup, and I've completely abandoned any semblance of a healthy diet."

He was about to banter back, when Bonita suddenly started to run in a circle, screaming about a bee.

"Is it on me?" She was swiveling her head around from one direction to the other, trying to look behind her.

Gabe walked over to her to inspect the parts of her back that she couldn't see. "It was just a little ol' honeybee."

"You don't understand! Those little suckers hunt me down and sting me wherever I am! I'm not paranoid. They come after me *in particular*. I was stung three times last summer! You laugh, but it's true."

"Well, he's gone now," Gabe reassured her. "They weren't bothering me."

"Well…maybe you just aren't as sweet as I am."

Gabe opened the passenger door for her and gave a little tip of his cowboy hat. "There's no denying that."

## Chapter Four

"Okay," Bonita announced after taking a shower, changing her clothing and putting on some makeup. "Now I actually feel like a normal human again."

After five more hours of travel, during which she was subjected to the full Willy Nelson catalog, they arrived at an equestrian facility in Grimes, Iowa. Considering the name of the town, Bonita was pleasantly surprised by the accommodations for Val. The stalls were a generous size and well maintained. There was a separate turnout paddock for Val, so she could be assured that he wouldn't get injured trying to figure out his position in the herd hierarchy.

Once they got Val unloaded and settled and after they cleaned the mobile stall, which gave Bonita a chance to work off some of her junk food calories, Gabe found an overnight spot to park the rig. Part of the living area expanded outward with a simple push of a button, adding additional square footage to the kitchen and sitting area. The rig had solar panels on the roof, so Gabe could park the rig away from electrical hookups. He had found a spot to park the rig that would allow them to see Val in his paddock.

Gabe was sitting at the dining table, a table that resembled a booth in a diner with bench seats on either side. Bonita slid into the bench opposite Gabe, feeling refreshed and awake for the first time that day.

"What's the plan for dinner?" she asked. In her family, food was important and meals were meant to be an event.

Gabe put down his phone and looked at her. Every time their eyes met and held, she was struck by how clear and blue the cowboy's eyes were. She couldn't always see them, for the brim of his hat, but when she did, it was a moment that lingered in her mind. There was a raw honesty there. And a kindness that always surprised her. She supposed she had a set opinion of men who wore cowboy boots and hats, and it wasn't, upon reflection, a positive one. Gabe was, little by little, changing that opinion.

"I usually stock what I need." He paused a second and then added, "I wasn't expecting company."

Bonita felt an immediate pang of guilt. She should apologize for barging in on the trip. She'd always had a difficult time apologizing—even when she knew she was squarely in the wrong, like now. The words *I'm sorry* just couldn't find their way to her lips. Instead, she stood up, went over to the kitchen cabinets and started to assess the situation. After scouting the refrigerator and the cabinets, Bonita, who had been cooking since she was young, already had several dishes in mind that she could make for dinner.

"You have ingredients for fajitas, a breakfast burrito or steak and eggs," she said as she wound her long, damp hair into a knot on the top of her head and secured it with a ponytail holder from the front pocket of her jeans. "What's your pleasure?"

Gabe looked at her like he was caught off guard by her offer. "I have all that in there?"

"Yes. You actually do." She laughed, feeling happy for some unfathomable reason. "You don't cook?"

"I grill."

"Of course. Well, I cook. Love to, actually. So let me make you dinner. It would feel like I'm being useful. What's your pleasure?"

"Steak and eggs sounds good."

"Coming right up," she said with a smile. "How do you like your steak cooked?"

"Just barely dead, I suppose."

"Rare it is."

Gabe went out for a bit to speak with the manager of the facility. While he was gone, Bonita hummed while she located all of the cooking essentials she would need to deliver on the promised meal. While the steak was broiling in the oven, she found plates and silverware and set the table.

It made her feel content to be cooking, even in such a tiny kitchen. Cooking had been her connection to her family in Mexico—all of her aunts and uncles and grandparents and cousins on her father's side, most of whom still lived in Mexico, had taught her how to cook authentic Mexican food. Her mother, whose family was of European descent, hadn't even known how to cook when she met Bonita's father. But before Evelyn became ill, she could cook a wide variety of traditional Mexican dishes, the kind that always brought a smile to George's face.

Bonita was just finishing the eggs when Gabe returned.

"Sorry about that." He took his hat off and hung it on a hook just inside the door. "They've got a horse they wanted me to look at."

"I've been having a good time." She turned the burner off and took the pan with the scrambled eggs off the stove. "I hope you like scrambled. I forgot to ask."

"I'm not too picky." Gabe sat down at the table. "That smells good enough to eat."

"Well. I hope you like it."

She made them both a plate and then joined him at the table. She knew from traveling with him that he was going to want water with no ice in his glass, so she had already taken care of that. Bonita already regretted the soda she had consumed, so she switched to water as well.

"This is the first real meal that's been cooked in that kitchen," Gabe told her.

She waited for him to take the first bite of steak, to give her a stamp of approval for the dinner, before she began to eat her portion of the scrambled eggs.

"Now, that's good," he said with a satisfied little smile. Her mother always said that a way to a man's heart was through his stomach. So far, Bonita believed her mother was right about that. "Where's your steak?"

"I don't eat meat."

"You don't meet very many vegetarians in Montana."

"You don't meet very many vegetarians in my family!" Bonita countered. "My father thinks it's sacrilegious to not eat meat, and trust me, none of my relatives in Mexico get it."

Gabe cut a tiny piece of steak for Tater, who had been waiting, ears perked forward, at the cowboy's feet.

"Is that who taught you to cook like this?"

Bonita nodded while she washed some eggs down with water. She wiped her mouth off with a napkin and then said, "Cooking and food is a big part of our culture. My mom didn't know how to boil water when she met my dad, but she learned quickly. I've been cooking since I was a kid."

"Well, you're dang good at it. It's rare for me to have a home-cooked meal on the road and it's been two nights in a row for me this time around. So I thank you."

"It was my pleasure. It's the least that I could do seeing as I'm technically a stowaway."

She meant those last words to be a roundabout way of apologizing. Gabe met her eyes, but he didn't pick up on the cue and run with it. He just gave her a simple nod, as was his way she was discovering, and let the matter drop.

"I'd like to go check on Val after we've cleaned up," she said. "I saw one of the hands take him to the stable and I'd like to see how he's settling in to his stall."

Gabe dropped his crumpled-up napkin on his plate. "You cooked, I'll clean."

"Are you sure?"

"I got the better end of that deal. Go on and visit with Val."

Bonita took Gabe up on his offer and headed to the barn. She found Val in his designated stall at the end of the long aisle, eating hay.

"Hi, handsome boy." She opened his stall gate and held out her hand to him so he could begin to learn her scent.

"There's some grooming tools hanging on that hook if you want to use them," suggested one of the stable-hands mucking out a stall across the aisle.

"Thank you. I think I will."

Bonita grabbed a body brush; she was glad to finally have some time to bond with Val. But when she started to brush his neck, Val nipped at her, backed up into the corner of the stall to avoid her and swished his tail, a sign that he was resisting her.

"I know you don't think so now, Val." She fought through the nerves she always seemed to feel around her new horse and kept on brushing him, not letting him rule the moment. "But you are going to learn to love me."

She brushed his body, ignoring his grouchy attitude when she switched sides and asked him to move his feet. Then she combed his mane and his tail and finished by cleaning out each of his hooves. The entire time she worked on him, he tried to bite her, and his body language, from the tail swishing to stomping his hind hooves, was a sign that he had some behavior issues that they were going to have to work on.

"You look super handsome now, Val." Bonita wrapped her arms around the horse's neck and gave him a quick hug. "I'll see you tomorrow. At a ridiculously early hour."

While she was putting the grooming tools back in the bucket hanging outside the stall, Bonita heard Gabe's voice nearby. She walked toward the sound of his voice.

He was standing next to what looked to be a full-blooded Thoroughbred in the large, indoor riding arena. He was talking to a couple of people who Bonita assumed to be the owners. She looked around and found that there were empty bleachers nearby. She climbed up to the midpoint in the bleachers and sat down.

"Everything we do with horses is pressure," Gabe was saying. "We put a halter on them, it's pressure. We ride them, it's pressure. What they want is to be left alone and eat. That's not how it's going to be for them, but we have to understand what they want if we're going to change their behavior. What is that you want this horse to be able to do?"

The younger of the two women, the one wearing a pair of riding breeches, said, "I want him to not freak out every time he sees a flag. When I take him to a show, he's fine, unless there's a flag. Then all bets are off. He bolts, he tries to buck me off…"

"Well, he might have had someone train him wrong with a flag. We don't know his history. So his reaction, at least to him, could make perfect sense, even if it's doesn't make perfect sense to you. But don't worry, we can work on it. We need to operate on the principle of pressure. Operating on the principle that horses respond to the application or the release of pressure, we can desensitize this horse to stimuli. In this case, a flag." Gabe nodded his head toward the other side of the arena. "Why don't the two of you stand over there so when he reacts, you won't be in the way, and I'll show you what you can do with him."

In Gabe's free hand, he was holding a training device that looked like a long crop with a flag on the end. He had the flag grasped in his hand, so the Thoroughbred didn't see it. Calmly, as was the way Gabe seemed to operate in the world, he stepped away from the horse, gave him some length of the lead rope and then showed the horse the flag.

The moment the horse spotted the flag, it started to rear and then buck and tried to run away. Gabe held on to the horse, and instead of taking the flag away, he waved the flag to keep the horse moving.

"If he's not doing what I want him to do, which is stand still, I keep him moving," Gabe explained while he worked. "In the horse world, whoever moves the feet is the boss. That's the way it goes. All this horse is looking for is a leader. That's what a horse is looking for in all of us."

When the horse finally stopped moving and stood still, Gabe dropped the flag to the ground. For the next thirty minutes, Gabe worked with the Thoroughbred, repeating the steps over and over again, until the horse let him rub the flag over his body.

"We don't want to teach him that this tool is another thing to fear, so we want to rub him all over his body with it to let him know that it's not."

Bonita heard one of the women say, "I've never seen him do that before. I can't believe that Gabe managed to accomplish in thirty minutes what we haven't been able to accomplish in all these years."

The women went out into the arena to thank Gabe and shower their horse with praise. The Thoroughbred was winded but calm in the presence of the flag. Gabe handed the woman in the riding breeches the lead rope. And then he handed her the training flag. "Now you have a flag."

Bonita met Gabe at the bottom of the bleachers and they walked side by side toward the rig. It was getting dark and she already knew that Gabe would be expecting to leave at 4:00 a.m.

"That was impressive." She glanced over at him, seeing the cowboy in a fresh light.

"Thank you."

"I didn't know you were a horse trainer."

He laughed a bit. "That's how I make my living, for the most part."

She had assumed, wrongly, that Gabe was only a long-distance horse transporter. He was so much more than that. She had been around trainers all of her life, but she'd never seen anyone work with a horse quite in that manner and she said as much.

"Horsemanship training is different, but it's the most important. Did you ever see that movie *The Horse Whisperer*?"

She nodded.

"I trained with Dennis Reis out in California. He was one of the trainers who worked on that movie." Gabe tipped his hat at a group of women standing in the tack room. "I had to go out there for a month and I had to take my own horse. But it was worth it. My career's been growing ever since."

"It doesn't seem like there'd be too much business in Bozeman."

"No." He smiled. "You're right about that. I train local when I can, but I spend most of my time traveling. I go down to Wellington in Florida during the summer. Folks have a lot of money to spend on training for their horses down there and they like to have me around."

"I can see why." She nodded. "I've never had that kind of training and it seems like I've been training on horseback for years."

"It's the foundation. That's where horse ownership

should start. Ride the horse from the ground, then get on his back."

When they got back to the rig, Gabe opened the door for her, as he was wont to do, and then followed her inside. The kitchen was clean and he had already pulled out the queen-size bed that had been tucked away inside of the convertible couch.

"You'll sleep here."

When she had first decided to join the trip unannounced, she imagined that there would be an opportunity for her to get a hotel room. Just like with the food plan, she hadn't really thought the entire scenario through. Why, after all, would Gabe spend all of this money on a decked-out rig like this only to spend money on a hotel room? It didn't make sense. But sleeping in the same space with him hadn't been a part of her original consideration. Her father had brought up the subject of the sleeping arrangement, but she had brushed off the concern.

"I hate to take your bed."

"You're not. I bunk up there." He pointed to the bunk bed above the front cabin. "I've never had this bed out before."

Gabe suggested that he take the first turn in the bathroom so he could get up in the bunk and pull the curtain. His attempt to give her some privacy, to make her more comfortable in an uncomfortable situation she had designed for herself, made her add a brick to the wall of respect she had been building for the cowboy day by day.

While he was in the bathroom taking a shower, she called her parents and checked in with her friends on social media. She had been posting pictures from her trip along the way and all of her friends loved Val. But the subject all of her female friends seemed to love even more was Gabe. Bonita scrolled through the comments, and almost to a person, there were questions about the "sexy cowboy."

Was Gabe sexy? He did have incredible blue eyes; there was no denying that. And it was true that there was something compelling about a man in a cowboy hat. And the way he was able to train horses was definitely a selling point. In fact, when she checked out Gabe's social media, ten to one of his contacts were women from the horse community.

"There's enough hot water for you."

Gabe opened the door to the bathroom, followed by a billow of steam. His wet hair was slicked back from his face and he was fully dressed down to his cowboy boots. He didn't look like a man about to go to bed.

"Okay." Bonita was sitting cross-legged on the bed.

Gabe stopped at the foot of the bed. "You want to keep Tater with you?"

Tater was curled up next to her leg. "She's comfortable."

Gabe nodded and then grabbed a ladder that was hanging on the wall and hooked it just beneath the bunk.

"I'm going to pull the curtain, so you'll have some privacy."

"I appreciate it. Thank you."

"I'm setting the alarm for three. We've got another ten to do tomorrow."

"I know." That was said with a tinge of sullenness.

"We've got to fold up that bed and get the extension back in place and move the rig so we can load Val."

"I'll be up. I promise."

Satisfied that he'd prepared her for the inevitable

early departure, the cowboy climbed up the ladder and disappeared behind the curtain.

Knowing that the alarm was going to go off sooner than she wanted, Bonita climbed off the bed, went into the bathroom and quickly prepared herself for bed. She cut her nightly routine in half, and dressed in a sweatshirt and sweatpants, she hurried over to the bed and got under the covers. Tater repositioned herself closer to her once she turned off the light.

It was hard to imagine for her, because she had insomnia, but the cowboy was already asleep, based on his breathing. With a sigh, Bonita kissed Tater on the head and prayed for sleep. Although she was beginning to adjust to the routine, life on the road was certainly not for her.

Gabe awakened thirty minutes before his alarm was set to go off. He'd taken his boots off but decided to sleep in his jeans and his shirt. In case of an emergency, he didn't want to be jumping out of the bunk in his socks and underwear. But it wasn't comfortable to sleep fully dressed and he hadn't slept as well as he'd like with ten hours of driving in his future. And yet he knew that it wasn't just his clothing that was making it difficult to sleep.

He had Bonita on the brain. From the moment he saw her, he'd wanted to ask her out. It was her attitude, initially, that had scared him off. It seemed like she was looking down on him and he didn't like anybody looking down on him. Little by little, she'd been changing his mind.

He liked her without her makeup, when she was teasing him, when she was cooking him a meal and when she was watching him train a horse like she respected him. And he liked it when she was fresh out of the shower, her long hair loose around her pretty face. The smell of her hair and her skin seemed to be everywhere—that faint scent of lavender.

She was his client, but he wanted to ask her out on a date.

She was his client, but he really wanted to kiss her.

He didn't usually date his clients. In truth, he hadn't dated much over the years. He'd been building his business and avoiding entanglements and fresh heartbreak. But there wasn't a rule against it. And technically, once he delivered Val, Bonita wasn't going to be his client any longer.

If he asked her out on a date, would she say yes? He'd never dated someone like Bonita; he was tempted to try.

Maybe when they got back to Bozeman and Val was safe in his new home, he was going to have to gather up the nerve to ask Ms. Delafuente to do him the honor of joining him on a date.

## Chapter Five

"Rapid City, South Dakota, here we come!" It was five past four in the morning, and Bonita, running on two hours of sleep and a strong cup of coffee, was sitting cross-legged in the passenger seat, waving good-bye to Grimes, Iowa.

"Thank you again for finding those creamers for me," she said to Gabe, who, as he always did, looked ·put together and prepared for the day—boots on, cowboy hat on and button-down shirt tucked in tight.

She saw him nod in the dark in response to her thank-you. He might be thinking it was a mistake to find those creamers in the lounge at the equestrian facility. Now that she had coffee, the caffeine was making her chatty.

"Hey!" Bonita exclaimed when she started to explore sightseeing in Rapid City on her phone. "Mount Rushmore is in Rapid City, South Dakota. Did you know that?"

Another nod.

"I've always wanted to see Mount Rushmore. I'm not kidding. I wonder if we'll have time. Do you think we'll have time?"

Gabe had told her during dinner the night before

that they would be staying with one of his father's long-time business partners. A friend of the family might be willing to lend them a car for a quick trip to Mount Rushmore.

"Have you been to Mount Rushmore?"

Gabe shook his head no.

"Do you *want* to see Mount Rushmore?"

He sighed a little. "If we get there in time, I'll see if Bill will lend me one of his vehicles and I'll take you there. That's not a problem."

She barely got her thank-you out before he turned on the music. Then she wished she hadn't had the coffee, which made her too talkative, which made him turn on the music, and now she couldn't fall asleep because she was too wired with caffeine.

*No bueno.* Not good at all.

Perhaps it was a form of self-preservation, or perhaps it was a form of indoctrination, but she actually caught herself singing along to a Trace Adkins song. The fact that she actually knew the words in the first place was cause for concern, but it was downright troublesome that she had, without thought, started to sing the words out loud.

"You don't like to talk much when you drive, do you?" she asked over the music.

Gabe seemed to be in the zone, focused on the road and not appearing to feel the need to talk. But thankfully, in response to her question, he switched off the music.

*¡Gracias a Dios!* She said a private thanks to God for answering her prayers. Better late than never.

"I don't usually have anyone to talk to. I've tried to have a conversation with Tater a time or two, but she's the quiet type."

Bonita smiled down at the dog in her lap; Tater had made all the difference for her on this trip. She was going to miss her when the trip was over. "Is that true, *perrita*?"

"It's nice to see her take to someone."

"I was just thinking how much I'm going to miss her. If you ever need a Tater-sitter, you just let me know."

That made him laugh. He had a nice laugh. And in truth, he had a nice smile.

"I can't believe I've done the things I've done these last three days," she mused aloud. "I've never seen the country this way. It's beautiful. Truly beautiful."

This was the closest thing to roughing it she had ever done in her life and although she wouldn't want to repeat it anytime soon, it had been an experience to travel this way.

"Rapid City is the capital of South Dakota, isn't it?"

"No. It's Pierre."

"Pierre? No. That doesn't sound right."

"Look it up."

"I will."

"But it's Pierre. I can name every capital of every US state."

Bonita searched for the capital of South Dakota on her phone.

"Shoot."

"It's Pierre, right?" he asked.

"Lucky guess."

"No. I'm telling you. I can name every capital. Quiz me."

"Hold on. I'm horrible at geography, so I have to find a resource."

She began to quiz Gabe, and every state she named, he came up with the correct capital without hesitation.

"Okay—here's one you won't get. Rhode Island."

"Providence."

"How did you *know* that?" She half laughed, half exclaimed.

"I'm a smart guy."

Gabe went on to name the rest of the capitals in the United States, including US territories and then just to show off, named the European capitals as well.

"Do you want me to move on to Africa?" he asked smugly.

"No, *gracias*!" She put her phone down. "I think I'll just assume you know the rest. And don't be offended, but I did judge the hat."

"I know you did," Gabe told her. "It wasn't the first time and it won't be the last."

Yesterday, it had sunk in that a cowboy like Gabe could be sexy. Jeans and cowboy boots, country music and four-wheel-drive trucks had never been her kind of sexy in a man. But what he did yesterday with that Thoroughbred. *That* was sexy. And as it turned out, he was also a smart cowboy. She had just assumed that he hadn't gone to college and maybe he hadn't. Either way, he wasn't dumb.

At the halfway mark, they made a pit stop, grabbed some lunch, gave Val some fresh hay and then headed out. Gabe didn't mess around and she had learned to appreciate that about him. He was focused and goal oriented. Maybe they didn't have the same type of goals, but they did have that personality trait in common.

They rode in silence for a while, and her mind, as it often did, drifted to her mother's illness. Her own life had been charmed up until that diagnosis—she had earned two bachelor's degrees, a master's degree and she had been accepted to medical school. She had worked for senators, she had traveled all over the world, and she had shown horses at some of the biggest venues in the country.

And, then her mother was diagnosed with ALS and everything, *everything*, changed. It was her mother's dream to retire to a horse ranch in Montana. And when her parents realized that retirement age was never going to come for one of them, George bought the horse ranch outside of Bozeman. Now Bonita was living in Bozeman, too. Taking care of her mother, managing the medical staff, making doctor appointments, arranging therapy and filling prescriptions had become her full-time job. Her father, her hero, was in many ways unable to handle his wife's steady decline.

"Do you know what just occurred to me?" An idea came into Bonita's head and she couldn't believe it had taken her so long to have it.

"What's that?"

"You train horses."

Gabe looked over at her, kind of curious, while she continued.

"I saw what you did with that horse last night. It was amazing."

"I don't know about amazing. It's just releasing the pressure at the right time so the horse knows what you want, is all."

"Do you think that you could teach my mom's horse to accept her wheelchair?"

Gabe didn't take much time to think about it. "I reckon I could."

Bonita turned her body toward him as much as she could with the restriction of the seat belt, her eyes welling up from a mixture of sadness and hope.

"Gabe. If you could, you have no idea what that would mean to me. What that would mean to my mom! All she wants to do is visit with Jasmine, to give her a treat, to pet her nose or brush her a little. But Jasmine is petrified of the wheelchair and Mom can't do without it anymore."

She took in a deep breath to steady herself before she continued.

"Montana was my mom's dream. To be in Montana with her horse. And now, she doesn't even go into the barn because she doesn't want to scare Jasmine. She only watches Jasmine graze from the window. It makes me feel…"

Bonita lowered her head and shook it, pausing to collect herself. "*Muy triste.* Very sad."

"I can't promise anything, Bonita," Gabe said. "But I can promise that I'll do my best."

"Thank you, Gabe." Her voice wavered. "It would be a gift to my mother that no amount of money could buy."

As she had prejudged Gabe, so, too, had she prejudged South Dakota. There were many things that she had gotten right—there were more wide-open spaces and trees than people. But she had wrongly assumed that only country folk, in small cabins they built with their own hands, lived in the Dakotas. On that front, she was mistaken.

Just on the outskirts of Rapid City, Gabe turned onto a drive leading up a steep hill that led to a sprawling structure constructed of logs. The house abutted a cliff overlooking Spring Creek Canyon. Even by Montana standards, this was a big house.

"I'm curious about the inside," she told Gabe.

"You'll see it." He drove past the house and followed a narrow road to the barn. The barn was a mini replica of the house, built with the same logs and aesthetic as the house.

Unlike the other stops, there wasn't anyone there to greet them. And there weren't any other horses in sight.

"They got out of the horse business years back. Bobbi has a couple of miniature donkeys, so I think Val will be okay here for a night. Let's give Tater a quick bathroom break and then put her back in the rig so we can get Val unloaded."

At the other stops, there was always another person to handle the Oldenburg. Today, Bonita needed to step up and handle her horse. It didn't set well with her that she felt uneasy around Val, especially when that had never happened to her before with any other horse.

Val came off the ramp full of energy and anxiety—his eyes were wide-open as he looked around at his strange surroundings, snorting and pawing at the ground. He refused to stand still, moving from one side to the other, while Gabe worked to get his shipping boots off.

"This is the last stop before home," she told Val and he thanked her by nipping at her.

She was relieved to get the lead rope off him and let him go in the pasture. She and Gabe leaned against the fence and watched the Oldenburg race around the pasture, bucking and working out his pent-up energy.

"He is a gorgeous horse." She spoke her thoughts aloud.

"That he is."

"But he hates me."

"It's not in a horse to hate you."

She looked at Gabe's profile. In a pretty short amount of time, she had come to respect his knowledge of horses. And it would do her spirit a world of good to think that he was right about this one.

"Is that true?"

"Sure it is." Gabe turned his clear, blue eyes toward her. "There's only two things horses are taught by their mamas. One, you eat grass. And two, everything else eats you. A horse is sensitive to our energy. They have to be. That's how they know if you're dangerous. If you're nervous around them, they are going to automatically put you in the predator category and they're going to do their best to get the heck away from you. That's instinct working for them and we can't fault them for doing what comes natural."

What Gabe was saying made sense. For some reason, she had always been nervous around Val and he was viewing her as a predator. She was going to have to work on that.

"He's fine for now," Gabe said, once Val had settled in the pasture and started to graze. "I'll come back and clean out the rig later. Do you still want to see Mount Rushmore?"

"That would be a *yes*."

"Then let's grab Tater and get going. I promised Bobbi that I'd have us back in time for some shindig they're having at the club."

"I didn't bring anything to wear to an event."

"Trust me. Bobbi will have you covered," Gabe said with certainty. "Once you meet her, you'll get it."

\* \* \*

When Gabe and Bonita returned from their trip to Mount Rushmore, Bobbi and her husband, Bill, had arrived home. Once Bonita met Bobbi, Gabe's cryptic comment made perfect sense.

Bobbi was her kind of woman—she wore nice jewelry even when she was wearing jeans, her makeup was flawless no matter the time of day, her nails were perfectly shaped and polished, the hair was on point, and the boots looked to be from Gucci's new fall collection. Bobbi was bringing some cosmopolitan flair to South Dakota. Bobbi could just as easily be getting ready for lunch on Rodeo Drive instead of standing in the rustic-motif kitchen of her South Dakota mansion.

"It's the views." Bonita was on the tour of the house with Bobbi while Gabe and Bill went out to get Val settled in the barn.

She was standing in a room, overlooking a canyon, with floor-to-ceiling windows. The house, built by Bill's family in the early 1920s, was ten thousand square feet of rustic masculinity. Heavy wood beams crossed the tall ceilings; the cabinets in the kitchen and bathrooms were dark knotted wood. For a house so large, it was unusually dark and cave-like. But then you would find yourself in a room with a wall of windows, and the glorious world outside was laid at your feet.

"It is all about these views," Bobbi agreed as she linked her arm with Bonita's. "But sometimes, I'd give anything to trade that view with a view of Bloomingdale's."

That made Bonita laugh. She was glad that she wasn't the only one who thought that way. "Gabe said that you grew up in Los Angeles?"

"Beverly Hills, 90210," Bobbi said, but it didn't come off as pretentious. "It was *fabulous*. The shopping and the dining."

"That's a long way from here," Bonita said wistfully, thinking of how far away Bozeman seemed to be from her stomping grounds in Washington, DC.

"It was an adjustment," her hostess confessed. "Who am I kidding? I'm still adjusting. But when I met Bear…"

Bobbi called her husband *Bear* and claimed that everyone did, but Bonita intended to stick with *Bill*.

"…my life changed. If you love someone as much as I love that man, you make it work. His great-grandfather built this home. It's meaningful to him, so there you go."

Bobbi led Bonita to her daughter's suite of rooms. "I know you weren't expecting to get dolled up, but the club is having this big, swanky event for the board of directors, and it's going to be *fabulous*. We have an amazing chef, so the food will be to die for, the booze is free, and halfway through the night everyone will be dancing with their shoes off."

Bobbi threw open the doors to a walk-in closet the size of a bedroom. "You look to be about Georgina's size. Let's find you something *fabulous* to wear."

Bobbi said the word *fabulous* a lot, but in the case of her daughter's dress options, they were indeed fabulous. For a moment, Bonita was transported out of South Dakota and into a couture closet of a woman's dreams.

"Is this a Hervé Léger?" she asked excitedly.

Bobbi had given her carte blanche with her daughter's wardrobe, swearing that Georgina wouldn't mind. The two of them had been searching the sea of cocktail options when Bonita came across a silver, geometric bandage dress that spoke her name.

"Oh, now *that* would look *fabulous* on you. You have the curves to fill that out."

Bonita held the dress up in front of her body in the full-length mirror and, as if for the first time, noticed how shabby she looked. She was wearing a rumpled shirt, jeans and her hair was in a sloppy ponytail—homeless chic. How could she have been beaten down by this road trip in such short order?

"Are you sure your daughter wouldn't mind?"

"Not at all." Bobbi waved her hand. "I'm the clothes-horse. Most of this she bought just to humor me. Look. The one you picked out still has the tag on it."

Bonita took another look at her image in the mirror. She didn't want to pass up an opportunity to get dressed up, glam out her makeup and feel like herself again.

"What about the shoes?" she asked Bobbi.

"What size do you wear?"

"Seven and a half."

"My size!" Bobbi grabbed her hand. "Let's go find you the perfect pair."

Gabe did something on this trip that he'd never done before—he left his planned travel route, with a client, to go on an excursion. Not only did he deviate from his plan, he borrowed a friend's vehicle to do it. There was something about Bonita that made him want to do nice things for her—there was something about her that made him want to go a little out of his way.

And since he'd always wanted to see Mount Rushmore but had never taken the time to go, it was a win-win to take Bonita. They had stood together, quietly, soaking in the awe of the presidential carvings that were beyond what he had ever seen in pictures. To be able to experience the sheer enormity of the sculptures and the artisan skill it took to create the faces of presidents past was worth the detour. Seeing how happy Bonita was to visit one of her bucket-list monuments was a bonus.

The moment they returned to his friend's log cabin mansion, as Gabe affectionately thought of it, Bobbi whisked Bonita off for an all-inclusive tour of the house and grounds, as anticipated. Gabe had a chance to catch up with Bill while he cleaned out the back of the rig and prepared it for the last leg of the trip. Val was happy in the pasture, so Gabe decided to leave him out until after he returned for the evening.

"The limo will be here to pick us up at seven sharp," Bill reminded him for the fourth time. Bill was a mountain of a man, tall, broad-shouldered and barrel-chested, but he toed the line with Bobbi. And Bobbi liked to be on time.

"I'll be ready," Gabe promised.

The last time he had dressed up was at his brother Bruce's vow renewal. When he'd asked Bobbi about landing in Rapid City on the third leg of his trip, she was happy to have him as long as he agreed to attend their event at the club. So he'd dusted off his wedding suit and brought it along.

After he finished his work, double-checked on Val and fed Tater, Gabe got himself showered, shaved and gussied up. He was glad that in South Dakota it was still acceptable to wear a cowboy hat to a formal event. He'd feel naked without it.

Gabe was the first one ready, so he waited for the others in a room with lookout views of the canyon. He felt nervous to see Bonita and he couldn't pinpoint why. His palms were a little clammy and his heart was beating just a bit harder than normal. He felt hot around his uncomfortable collar.

"Bobbi sent me to find you."

At the sound of her voice ringing sweet in his ears, Gabe turned away from the windows. The sight of her, standing in a silver cocktail dress that hugged her hourglass curves, made him feel like someone had just walked over to him and punched him in the gut. She wore her hair down tonight, letting it cascade around her face and shoulders.

"This place is enormous." Bonita smiled at him as she walked his way. "I was afraid I wouldn't be able to find my way back."

The woman who had been a constant companion in his thoughts of late stopped in front of him and he breathed in that delicate, lovely signature lavender scent on her skin.

*Beautiful Bonita.*

"You look beautiful, Bonita."

He was awarded with a smile, drawing his attention to her perfectly red lips. "Thank you, Gabe. And may I say, you look very handsome in that suit."

In response, Gabe offered her his arm. As he escorted Bonita down to the awaiting car, for the first time in such a long time, the cowboy felt like he was on top of the world.

## Chapter Six

Bonita was clearly in her element at the formal country-club event. There was a social code, a language, that guided such events, and she evidently spoke that language fluently. Gabe, on the other hand, felt strung up tight like he was in a straitjacket and wished he could've worn his Wranglers. But as uncomfortable as he was from head to toe, it was worth the discomfort to escort Bonita into the room. She was a lovely beacon that drew the admiring looks of the men in the room and he felt as if he was walking with his head held just a little bit higher for having her on his arm.

Before they entered the main ballroom, Bonita leaned over and whispered, "This dress isn't too Kim Kardashian, is it?"

"No."

She glanced up into his face. "You do know who that is, right?"

"Yes. I know who that is."

The woman did really think he was completely out of touch with civilization. Now granted, he didn't know who the designer of her dress was, but that was a normal guy thing not to know, wasn't it?

"Look at this, Gabe. This is so much fun!" Bonita was all smiles as he held out her chair at their assigned table.

There was so much silverware on the table; Gabe knew he was in for a long, drawn-out meal. He considered himself to be on the job until Val was safely delivered to his new home, but he sorely wanted a scotch on the rocks.

"I love pink champagne!" His companion accepted a glass of champagne from a server, her sable-brown eyes flashing with happiness.

Bonita didn't sit still for long—she wanted to mingle and circulate and meet all of Bobbi's friends. Gabe decided to unstick himself from the chair and head over to Bill's small gathering of men. But he did like to keep track of Bonita, glancing around the room to find her every now and again.

Perhaps he had never really seen her in her natural habitat—a socialite event—because this Bonita was laughing and talking animatedly with her hands and showing one of Bobbi's friends a couple of salsa moves. It was difficult for him to reconcile the woman he was seeing now with the woman who looked adorably grumpy at four o'clock in the morning wearing an oversize sweatshirt and her face scrubbed clean of makeup.

When it was time for dinner to be served, Bonita arrived back at the table with a fresh glass of champagne.

"I love this place." She leaned toward him. "Everyone is so nice."

"I'm glad you're having a good time."

"I'm having a *fabulous* time." She drank a sip of champagne. "Will you pass me one of those rolls? I'm feeling just the slightest bit tipsy."

As he suspected, the amount of silverware was an omen of things to come. One course after another was served to the point that he got tired of the rotation of clearing and serving and cleansing his palate. The only real enjoyment he could find was watching Bonita blossoming next to him. In short order, she had managed to engage everyone at the table in conversation, and from what he could tell, the people of Rapid City had embraced his companion with open arms.

"Coffee means it's almost over." Gabe didn't mean to speak that sentiment aloud, but it came out of his mouth anyway.

Surprised, Bonita turned toward him. "Aren't you having a good time?"

He was sorry to hear the disappointment in her voice, but this wasn't his kind of party. "It's been a long day."

Concern for him flashed across the features of her pretty face. For the briefest of moments, she placed her warm, small hand over his. "Do you want to go home? I'm sure Bobbi can arrange for you to get a ride back."

He was exhausted and overstuffed with fancy food and his suit jacket was too constricting, but there was a young man on the other side of the room who hadn't been able to keep his eyes off of Bonita. If Gabe gave in to his exhaustion and discomfort, that young man might just move in on Bonita before he even had a chance to let his own intentions be known. So he stayed.

"I'm glad you're staying. I know you're tired, but I like your company."

Was that the champagne talking? Gabe didn't care. He liked what he was hearing.

"And they're going to have dancing soon. Do you dance?"

"No."

She looked disappointed again. "No?"

He shook his head and tried to make his lips form some sort of semblance of a smile and failed.

"Never?"

He shook his head.

"What about at your prom?" she persisted.

"No."

"Not even at a junior high school dance?"

Another shake of his head.

"Well." Bonita's red lips frowned in a very appealing way. "That's unfortunate. I really wanted to dance tonight."

"You wanted to dance with me?"

Their eyes met and held. "You're my date, in a manner of speaking."

Even though Gabe was of a mind to go out of his way for Bonita, dancing was not an option. He wasn't good at it. He didn't like to do it. And that was the final verdict on that subject.

At least, that was his final verdict until he spotted that young man, the one with saucer-eyes for Bonita, heading toward their table once the band was into the third song. Gabe discovered that he was standing up; and then he discovered that he was standing beside Bonita's chair, blocking the young man's path and holding out his hand.

"Would you like to dance?"

Her eyebrows rose and the smile was slow to come to her mouth, but she put her hand into his and stood up.

With his palm gently resting on the small of her back, Gabe followed Bonita out to the dance floor. Bobbi smiled broadly at them and waved her hand from the other side of the floor. The only saving grace of this situation was that the space was crowded with couples and there wasn't much room to move. That suited him just fine because in the dance moves department, he had an empty shelf.

"All I can do is sway," Gabe said as Bonita stepped into his arms.

She put one hand on his shoulder and held his hand with the other. "Just put your hand on my back and then we can sway together."

He had felt embarrassed to even try to dance with a woman, but his desire to keep Bonita to himself for the night had propelled him to do things he wouldn't ordinarily do. Once he was holding her in his arms, the fragrant smell of her skin enticing his senses, he couldn't understand why he hadn't rushed her to the dance floor the minute the music started.

"Thank you." She smiled up at him shyly. "I don't know what made you change your mind…"

"You." He wasn't sure why he gave such a nakedly honest answer, but he did. "You changed my mind."

After Bobbi and Bill said good-night, Bonita and Gabe walked down to the pasture to bring Val in for the night. The sky was clear and cloudless, with a three-quarter moon shining its yellow glow across the tops of the trees in the canyon. For Bonita, this short walk in the moonlight was the perfect ending to a perfectly wonderful evening.

"That was the best night I have had in…" A few feet away from the front doorstep of the log cabin mansion, Bonita leaned back her head, extended her arms and spun around in a circle. "Ever!"

With a tipsy giggle, she stopped spinning and nearly fell over instead. Gabe was there to catch her; she liked the feel of his warm, strong hands, so masculine and rough, on the cool skin of her arms.

*"Estoy un poco borracha."*

"I think so," he said, agreeing that she was a little drunk.

"Hey!" She hit his arm affectionately. "You *do* understand Spanish."

"I understood that well enough."

"Aren't you happy we came here?" At the front door, Bonita spun around to face her handsome cowboy escort. She'd had no idea how handsome Gabe truly was until tonight.

He was standing with his hands in his pockets as if he were challenging himself not to touch her at this moment that so inclined itself to a good-night kiss. Of course, this hadn't been a *true* date and he wasn't *really* her escort.

"We have an early morning tomorrow," he said. "I'll say good-night now."

"You always say that."

He smiled at her and seemed to be waiting for her to open the door so he could make his way back to the rig. "That's because it's always true."

She wasn't quite ready to say good-night. When she

said good-night, then the evening would be over and 3:00 a.m. was just around the corner.

"Do you always tell the truth, cowboy?"

A bemused expression flashed in his bright blue eyes. "More often than not."

"Do you want to kiss me?"

For her, tipsy and light-headed, it seemed like he took an awfully long time to answer that simple question.

"Yes. I do, Bonita."

Steadying herself by holding on to the lapels of Gabe's suit jacket, she stood up on her tiptoes and kissed him on the lips. It was a short kiss, but a kiss nonetheless. Gabe looked as shocked by it as she felt. Bonita let go of his lapels.

"Well, at least we got that out of the way." She reached for the door and opened it. With one last glance at the seemingly confused cowboy, Bonita said goodnight and closed the door.

Inside, she leaned back against the door to steady herself. That champagne must have gone straight to her head, because she wasn't some carefree coed on spring break in Daytona Beach.

And yet, quite unexpectedly, she had just kissed a cowboy.


"Could we please not listen to this music right now? Please? I beg of you. If I hear one more country artist singing about one more country problem, I'm going to sincerely lose my mind."

According to the map on Bonita's phone, they were only an hour away from Bozeman and then it would be a short thirty-minute trip to her family's ranch. She had awakened at 3:00 a.m. and hit the snooze button twice before dragging herself out of the warm, comfy bed. That champagne had tasted so good going down, but it had left her with the worst hangover she had experienced in years. She had thankfully managed to fall asleep soon after they left Bobbi and Bill's log cabin estate but had been rudely awakened by Blake Shelton.

Gabe turned off the music and then the ride was quiet for several miles.

"Bill gave me some bags of deer corn. I was thinking of giving a couple to your father if you think he'd like them."

"We both love to feed the deer. I can't wait until we have babies."

"I'll leave you a couple of bags, then."

After a pause, she asked suspiciously, "You aren't going to use yours to lure the deer onto your property so you can shoot them, are you?"

"It's not hunting season."

"Well—that's not an answer."

"I hunt, if that's what you're getting at."

"I will *never* understand why someone would want to kill a beautiful living creature."

"There are only certain times of the year that we harvest," he said instead of addressing her comment directly.

"By harvesting, you mean killing."

He didn't respond to that.

"Look," Bonita said, "we aren't going to agree on this. I'm a vegetarian. So you and I are just going to have to agree to disagree on this one. I've decided to like you anyway."

That made him smile.

After another couple mile markers in silence, Gabe asked, "So you don't like country music?"

"Now that we're almost home, I can tell you how much I sincerely hate the genre. I didn't want to mess with your driving mojo, but for goodness' sake! I have country lyric earworms that are driving me insane. Last night, I dreamed I was singing with the Judds."

"It's the only music I listen to."

"Trust me. I know."

"So I listen to country music and I hunt. That's two strikes against me."

She looked at him and he looked back for a brief second before he put his eyes back on the road.

"I intend to spend the rest of my life in Montana."

"I intend to move back to civilization as soon as possible."

"I'm a Republican."

"Okay, now that's truly shocking," she scoffed. "Please. We're in *Montana*. You wear a cowboy hat. You drive a truck."

"Let's put aside the blatant stereotyping for a minute. I bet you're, what…a socialist?"

"I am a progressive, thank you very much. I just happen to want to move our country forward instead of taking us back to the 1950s like some people!" By the end of her statement, she had raised her voice a little.

In turn, Gabe raised his voice a notch. "You kissed me last night."

"I know that," she snapped at him. "I was there!"

Gabe paused for a split second and then he said, "I think we should go out."

She had been prepared to fire back at him, but he

completely changed direction on her, catching her off guard.

"You're asking me out. On a date?" Perplexed, Bonita turned her body toward him. "You think I'm a tree-hugging elitist!"

"And you think I'm a deer-murdering hillbilly."

That made her start laughing and when she laughed it made her headache worse. "Ow." She held her head in her hands.

Gabe was laughing now, too.

"For some strange reason, I do seem to enjoy your company." She leaned her head back on the headrest and smiled at him.

"And I enjoy yours." He glanced over at her with those clear, blue eyes that always struck a chord somewhere deep within her. "So go out with me."

Maybe it would do her some good to get out a little. It had been depressing moving to Bozeman with only managing her mother's illness to keep her mind occupied.

"Just as friends, though," Bonita said after a moment of thought.

"We'll just be two friends hanging out in the same place."

He had a way of making her laugh, and she hadn't felt like laughing all that much lately. "Okay." She nodded with a small smile. "I'll go out with you."

She sent her father a text letting him know that they were pulling onto the winding driveway. George was standing just outside of the barn entrance, awaiting their arrival. Bonita was always so happy to see her father, and she was anxious to see her mother again. But there was a knot in her stomach as Gabe pulled up the stable. She had managed, for the most part, to leave all of the stress and demands of her mother's illness behind for the last few days. And now that reprieve was over.

*"Mija!"* George enveloped her in a bear hug and kissed her on each cheek.

"We made it." She hugged him tightly for a moment longer before letting him go.

"Sir." Gabe held out his hand to her father.

"Thank you for bringing them home safely," her father said, and Bonita could tell by the way he interacted with Gabe that the cowboy had his respect.

Gabe gave a quick tip of his hat in response before he headed to the back of the rig to unload Val.

George's round face was beaming—he loved it when they acquired a new horse. She didn't have the heart to tell him that Val was displaying some behaviors that would have to be remedied, probably with Gabe's help.

Val, in all his dappled-gray glory, was anxious to get out of the rig. Once he was free of the mobile stall, Val tossed his head, snorted and pawed at the ground.

"Look at him!" George always accented his words with his hands. "He's incredible!" Her father, in his excitement, came over to her and put his arm around her shoulders. "Look, *mija.* Your dream! He is here!"

Once again, Bonita hugged her father. *"Gracias, papá."*

George kissed her on the forehead and then took the lead rope from Gabe. "What do you think of this horse, Gabe?" her father asked loudly.

"I like him."

After Gabe took off the shipping boots one last time, George led Val over to one of the large pastures and let the Oldenburg free. Her mother's horse, Jasmine, was in the adjacent pasture, so they would have a chance to get acquainted. The one thing that did make Bonita happy was the fact that Jasmine wouldn't be alone any longer. It wasn't natural for horses to live alone, and Jasmine needed an equine companion.

"This is wonderful!" Her father threw up his hands with a wide smile. "This is her dream and I have made it come true!"

Gabe was closing up the back of the rig out of earshot. "How is Mom?" Bonita asked.

Her father's smile faltered a bit. "Let's talk in a minute."

Her heart seized. "Has something happened?"

"In a minute." He waved her off.

George took a wad of cash out of his pocket and walked over to Gabe. He pressed the money into the cowboy's hand with another thank-you.

"Gabe is going to help us acclimate Jasmine to Mom's wheelchair, Dad."

"*Perfecto!* This is a very big problem for us." George then turned away with a wave. "*Mija*—I will see you inside. Your mother is so happy you're home."

Bonita picked Tater up after she had some time to roam in a nearby patch of grass. "I am going to miss you so much."

Tater licked her on the nose and then gently bit the tip, which made her laugh.

"Okay." She handed Tater to Gabe. "Time to say goodbye."

She couldn't have anticipated what it would have felt like to end the trip. She had begun the trip feeling suspicious of Gabe and his ability to handle a horse like Val. But she had been proved wrong on so many levels when it came to the cowboy. He was a kind man, talented, funny and smart. Over the last four days, they had begun a friendship. And she was going to miss him.

"Well." Gabe stood near the driver's door of his rig. "We got him here safe."

"You did."

They stood together in an awkward moment—there seemed to be something to say, but neither of them knew what that was.

"I'll text you." She finally broke the silence. "And we'll set up a time. For Jasmine, I mean."

Gabe climbed behind the wheel, rolled down the window, and their eyes met. He tipped his hat to her. "I'm going out of town for another transport. As soon as I get back, I'll be looking to cash in on that promise for dinner."

"And you'll work with Jasmine."

"And I'll work with Jasmine."

Bonita stood in the driveway watching him drive away. Inside, there was sadness, an odd sense of loss. Her adventure—one she hadn't expected to have—was over. And now it was time to return to her duties as her mother's advocate and her support system. It was a role she was honored to fill, but watching her mother lose her battle with a degenerative disease was also exhausting and sorrowful.

With one last wave as Gabe disappeared from view, Bonita turned away from the days spent on the road with the cowboy and walked quickly toward the house, worried about her father's evasive comments about her mother's condition.

## Chapter Seven

"**M**om!" Bonita made a beeline for her mother, who was sitting in the great room that overlooked the pastures. It broke her heart to realize that not only were her mother's days of riding over, but that she couldn't get close to her beloved horse because of the wheelchair.

*"Mija!"* There was a smile for her in her mother's eyes, but ALS, which systematically destroyed the muscles in the body, had robbed Evelyn of her smile.

The one word her mother said, *my daughter* in Spanish, had been spoken in nearly a whisper. Bonita knew that her mother was probably shouting it even to get that small sound out. Evelyn had a rare, aggressive form of ALS with a familial component that affected only 10 percent of patients with ALS. Evelyn's grandmother and great-grandfather had also died from complications related to ALS; after predictive genetic testing, Bonita now knew that she had also inherited the gene. Inheriting the gene didn't mean she would share the same fate as her mother, but it did mean that she could pass the gene down to any children.

Bonita pressed her cheek to her mother's, her eyes

scanning her for signs of change. The disease was so aggressive that there were changes in her mother's functioning day by day. She had been gone four days, and in that time, Evelyn's voice seemed softer, her breathing seemed shallower, and she looked thinner.

Bonita pulled a chair up next to her mother's wheelchair and took Evelyn's hand into hers.

"I've missed you." She kissed her mother's hand.

"I've missed you."

Bonita understood her mother's words, but someone who didn't know her wouldn't have. As the muscles in her mother's face and mouth failed, her speech became slurred and slow, like a tape that was running on the wrong speed.

Her mother's eyes shifted to the field where Val was grazing. "He's beautiful," she said.

Val was beautiful. But Bonita's doubts about the decision to bring a show horse to the ranch, a horse that needed to be kept on a strict riding and training program, had only intensified. She knew that her father wanted to neutralize some of her sadness over her mother's illness with a gift of her dream horse, but what her father didn't realize was that the idea of riding while Evelyn was bound to her wheelchair felt like she was being insensitive to her mother. Bonita had told her father as much when he surprised her with Val, but he had refused to budge on the purchase. Either way, Val was coming to Montana.

"Now you can show him," Evelyn added.

"Mom." Bonita shook her head. "I'm not going to keep leaving. Going to get Val was one thing. Leaving every weekend to go to shows is another."

"You need to live your life."

"I am living my life, Mom." She leaned down and kissed the back of her mother's hand once more. "*You* are my life."

They sat together in silence, just enjoying each other's company, until the nurse assigned to her mother in the afternoon returned from her lunch break.

"It's time for exercise, Evelyn." Kim joined them in the great room.

Bonita didn't want to let go of her mother's hand just yet, but having her mother's arms and legs manually exercised was important. When her mother and father had first moved to the ranch, which seemed like a lifetime ago instead of only a year, her mother could walk. Yes, she had a limp and there had been weakness in her arm, but she'd been independent. Now, only a year later, Evelyn was completely dependent with only limited use of her right hand and arm.

Bonita stood up and kissed her mother's cheek. "I'm going to unpack and then I'll come find you."

Evelyn used her right thumb to move her electric wheelchair. As her mother's condition worsened, her father made changes to the house to accommodate Evelyn's needs. Furniture had been rearranged and special equipment had been installed in a room on the first floor, which was now her mother's suite.

"Kim." Bonita got the nurse's attention. She lowered her voice a bit when she said, "Mom looks like she's lost some weight."

"Swallowing has been a challenge these last couple of days. We've been working on the techniques her therapist gave us, and that's helped a bit."

Her mother had been a little on the chubby side when she was first diagnosed but had lost weight in both muscle and fat along the way. They had managed to keep her stable for the last couple of months but decisions regarding a feeding tube were in their near future. So far, Evelyn had refused to even consider the option.

"Is there anything else I should know about?" she asked the nurse.

Kim's expression changed before she caught herself and set her expression back to neutral. "I think you'd better speak to your mom about that."

Instead of unpacking as she had planned, Bonita headed to her father's office on the third floor of the house.

Sitting behind a large, ornately carved executive desk, her father was on the phone. He smiled at her and waved her to sit down in one of the chairs opposite the desk. Instead, she walked to the enormous picture window overlooking the acres of pasture and the Montana mountains off in the distance.

Her stomach was upset. Her father had been cryptic when she first arrived home and alarm bells were going off in her head. After seeing her mother and speaking briefly with Kim, her sense that something had changed in her short absence had grown stronger.

"Why don't you sit down?" George asked in his booming voice. "And tell me about your trip."

Her arms crossed in front of her body, Bonita didn't sit. "Maybe later. I'm worried about Mom. She's lost weight. And when I asked Kim about it, she said that I should speak to Mom about it."

George's smile dropped. He sighed and rubbed his hands over his face several times before he threaded his fingers together, rested them on the desk and leaned forward.

Unsmiling, he said in a solemn tone, "There have been some decisions made, *mija*."

Bonita's stomach churned harder. "Decisions? What decisions?"

George pushed away from the desk, tucked his hands in his front pockets. "Let's go see Mom. This is her conversation to have with you."

"You are scaring me." Bonita's arms tightened around her body.

George crossed to her, put his arms around her and held her tightly. "I wish I had the words to make all of this go away."

But he didn't. No one did.

They went down to the first floor where Kim was just finishing her mother's range of motion exercises.

"We're all done here." Kim seemed to understand that the family needed privacy and left the room.

"Hello, my darling." George kissed his wife and took her hand in his.

*"Te amo,"* Evelyn said to her husband.

"And I love you." He kissed his wife's hand.

Evelyn and George had been in love for decades and their love seemed to be stronger now than ever before. It was hard to imagine her father's life without Evelyn. What would he do? Would he ever be happy again? Bonita didn't know the answers to those questions.

"It's time to tell your daughter," George said gently to his wife. "I'm right here."

Bonita stared at her parents as realization dawned. Her mother didn't have to say the words—in her heart she already knew what was coming.

"I don't want the ventilator." Her mother fought to get those words out.

Bonita's body felt frozen in place; she couldn't move, her legs felt numb, and she had to remind herself to take in a breath. Every patient with ALS had to make a decision about whether to breathe with the support of a ventilator when the muscles supporting the lungs failed. George and Bonita had both been lobbying for the ventilator because it meant extending Evelyn's life.

"I want nature to take its course now." Her mother paused to catch her breath before she added, "I'm ready."

Bonita screamed no in her mind but stuffed it down inside her gut. She knelt down beside her mother's wheelchair, tears on her cheeks, and took her mother's free hand in her own.

"Mom, *please.*"

"You have so much to do with your life, *mija.*"

"This is what I'm supposed to be doing with my life. Taking care of you!" Bonita looked up at her father. "Dad. Tell her."

"I have." George had a catch in his voice. "Many times. Many, many times."

"This…" Evelyn's breaths were shallow and her words came out in a whisper "…is my life. Respect my decision."

Bonita sat back on her heels with fresh tears on her face. She felt numb inside.

"What about the feeding tube?" she asked dully. "Are you going to refuse that as well?"

"I'm in God's hands," Evelyn told her, with a look of love and devotion, as always, for her Lord in her eyes.

The week following her return to the ranch had been a week of trials for Bonita. In order to keep her mother at home, they needed an around-the-clock crew of nurses to transfer her from bed to wheelchair, handle bathroom duties and help with feeding and dressing and exercising.

Bonita threw herself back into the management of the staff, the management of the ranch and trying to get Val settled in his new home. Whenever thoughts of her mother's end-of-life decisions rose to the surface of her mind, she swiped them away. There wasn't any use in dwelling on it. Evelyn had the right to decide and now it was up to Bonita to do her best to support her decision, no matter how much she disagreed.

"Good morning!" Her father startled her when he walked up to her.

She stopped brushing Val for a moment and hugged her dad. "Hi."

"How's he doing for you?"

Bonita shook her head in frustration. "He fights me every step of the way. He doesn't want to be brushed, he doesn't want to get his hooves picked, he doesn't want to be ridden. He tried to buck me off when I mounted yesterday. I called Candace and she's stunned. As far as she knows, they didn't have any trouble with him."

"Just give him some time. This is a big change for him." George rubbed the horse's neck.

"I know." She went back to brushing the tall horse. "I just wish that you'd listened to me about waiting to buy a show horse. I'm too busy with mom to train right now."

"That's exactly why this is the right time," her father argued. "You need to do something other than focus on your mother. No one doubts your devotion to her, but it's not healthy to never take a break. You need to take some time for yourself. When you hover, it upsets your mother. We were both happy to see you take some time for yourself and take a trip. It's healthy for you to get away. You know if your mother had it her way, you'd be back East in medical school."

Bonita dropped the brush in the bucket and grabbed a mane and tail comb. "I'm not leaving." She started to brush the tangles from Val's thick gray-and-white tail.

"You are your mother's daughter."

"That's true."

There were a couple of minutes of silence between them before her father broached a new subject. "Speaking of getting away. Your mother and I have decided that it's time for me to re-involve myself with the business."

Bonita stopped combing Val's tail and looked up at her father. "What does that mean?"

Her father's hands were in his front pockets. "Some traveling."

She straightened, tossed the comb in the bucket, and hands on hips, she shook her head in disbelief. "You're going to start traveling? *Now?*"

"You have everything under control here. I'm just staring at the walls with nothing to do. I'm not ready to be a retired person."

"Mom is dying." Bonita nearly choked on the words. "Every day there's a change for the worse. How can you leave her?"

There was a flash of anger mixed with sorrow in her father's brown eyes. He turned his face away from her, and when he looked back, she could see that his eyes were wet with unshed tears. She had never seen her father close to crying—not even when her mother was diagnosed.

"She is your mother, but she…" her father pointed toward the house "…is the love of my life. And I am *losing* her. Day by goddamn day, I'm losing her. And there's nothing I can do to stop it."

George sucked in a breath and blew it out. "This is torture. My Evelyn understands why I need to do something to occupy my time."

Wordlessly, Bonita crossed to her father and hugged him tightly. Maybe she would have been less understanding if she hadn't gone on that four-day trip with Gabe. That break had given her a boost of energy and a renewed perspective. Why should she begrudge her father the same time of respite from the stark reality of their lives?

"I'm sorry, Dad."

"No." George kissed her on the top of her head. "I'm sorry."

Gabe had another transport job after he delivered Val and when he returned to Bozeman the following week, the first order of business was going to see Bonita. He had received a distressed text from her while he was out of town and when he returned her call, he could tell that she needed him. So he rearranged his schedule a bit and made sure he could spend some extra time at the ranch with her.

"Gabe!" Bonita smiled at him in greeting and reached out to shake his hand. "Thank you for squeezing us in. I know you have a busy schedule."

There it was, the face that had been on his mind for the last week. He couldn't seem to get Bonita out of his head. He had missed her on his last transport gig, which was a huge surprise. He always loved traveling alone.

Yet after one trip with Bonita, traveling alone had lost some of its shine.

He accepted her hand, liking the way her slender fingers felt in his hand. Her hair was pulled back into one thick braid down her back and she still had that faint, sweet scent of lavender that tickled his senses. He did notice that even though her makeup was done, she had dark circles under puffy eyes, as if she hadn't been sleeping well or she'd been crying.

Like most owners with a problem horse, Bonita skipped the pleasantries and started to unload all of the issues she'd been having with the Oldenburg.

"I honestly thought that you were only going to be working with Jasmine, but Val has been much more than I bargained for."

"I'll work with him." He felt like he wanted to give her a hug—she looked like she might need one.

"Where should we start?"

"Let's work with your mom's horse first. You said something about this situation being time sensitive?"

Time sensitive was an understatement. Time was running out. The one gift Bonita could give her mom was time with Jasmine.

Jasmine had been six months old when Evelyn bought her; she'd trained her and then showed Jasmine for many years, and the Thoroughbred was one of the great loves of her life. Not being able to spend time with Jasmine was a constant source of sadness for Evelyn.

So much had changed from the first time Bonita had met Gabe. In the beginning, she had dismissed him as a backwoods cowboy. Now, she felt relieved to see his truck pull up next to the barn. He had a gift with horses and even though she had been riding since she was a kid, she'd never had any sort of horsemanship training. Val needed to learn how to respect humans when they were on the ground and on his back; the horse needed to have specific training to accept her as the head of his herd, and that was the kind of skill that a horseman like Gabe possessed. She needed him and she knew it now.

"This is Jasmine." Bonita crossed to the other side of the aisle to the Thoroughbred's stall. "She's twenty-two. My mom has had her since she was a baby, but she hasn't been able to spend any time with her lately because Jasmine is petrified of the electric wheelchair."

"Tell me what you've tried so far."

"We've tried several times with Mom in the wheelchair. I've tried just working with Jasmine and the wheelchair without Mom. For a while, we were using the manual chair, but it became too much for Mom. Transferring from the electric wheelchair to the manual just for a short visit with Jasmine was hard on Mom. And really, Mom wants to see Jasmine when she *wants* to see her, not when it takes an army of people to get her there."

Bonita had thought long and hard about introducing Gabe to her mother. Some people could be awkward around people in wheelchairs and were uncomfortable with her mother's speech. But it made sense that if Gabe was going to help them with Jasmine that he would need to get the entire picture.

"I was thinking that you could meet my mom, get a look at her wheelchair."

"All right."

Bonita walked with Gabe to the front door of the

house. She paused before opening it. "My mom can be difficult to understand. I'll translate for her."

If Gabe was surprised by her comment, it didn't show on his face as he took off his hat and smoothed his hair back from his forehead with his hand. It was endearing to see him make an attempt to look nice for her mom.

Evelyn was spending the morning in the great room, her favorite room in the house, and she was using her computer that she could control with her eyes. Danielle, the morning nurse, was sitting at the other end of the room, giving her mom some space but still within striking distance if help was needed.

"Mom." Bonita suddenly had a weird knot in her stomach at the thought of introducing Gabe to her mother. "This is Gabe Brand, the horse trainer I was telling you about. Gabe, this is my mom, Evelyn."

Bonita was very focused on Gabe's face as he extended his hand to her mother. Evelyn lifted her arm as much as she could so Gabe could take her hand. He didn't look uncomfortable around her mom at all, and it made Bonita like him even more.

"It's a pleasure to meet you, Evelyn," Gabe said in that country drawl of his that Bonita had begun to appreciate and even miss over the last week.

Bonita also introduced Gabe to the nurse and then she wanted to focus on the purpose of the trainer's visit. This was a working day for him and they needed to accomplish as much as possible on the first day.

"Do you think Jasmine will be able to get used to my chair?" Evelyn asked, the look in her eyes hopeful.

Gabe looked to Bonita for a translation and once he understood the question, he nodded. "Yes, ma'am. She'll get used to it. I've seen plenty of horses work with people in wheelchairs. We just have to figure out how to teach Jasmine her job. What do you want her to do?"

"I want to visit her while she's in her stall," Evelyn said. "And I want her to come up to me when I go to the fence. She used to always run up to see me when she was in the pasture."

"I believe we can get her there pretty quick," Gabe said and his confidence gave Bonita hope.

"Thank you," Evelyn struggled to say, her breath labored.

"It's my pleasure." Gabe put his hat back on his head and tipped the brim toward Evelyn. "I'd better get to it now."

Bonita gave her mom a quick hug and a kiss and Evelyn touched her hand.

*"Mija,"* her mother said with a renewed hope in her eyes. "I like him."

## Chapter Eight

Gabe first took Jasmine into the round pen and worked with her, asking her to back up, move her front feet and then move her hind feet on command. Next, he stood in the center of the pen and asked her to trot and then canter on command.

In all her years working with horses, Bonita had never seen anyone train a horse without a lunge line attached to the halter. All Gabe had was a training tool with a flag on the end and he rarely used his voice. It was like watching a dance—Jasmine would toss her head, pin back her ears as a sign of acting disrespectful, and Gabe snapped the flag sending the mare forward. If Jasmine slowed down, Gabe would lift the flag to ask her to speed up her pace. Sometimes he only moved toward the horse's hindquarter to put pressure on her and she increased her speed. Watching Gabe train a horse was mesmerizing—she never tired of it.

"Now that's not something you see every day." Bonita's father joined her at the round pen.

"It's amazing what Gabe can do with a horse," she told her father. "I've never seen anything like it. Just look at Jasmine—she's never been this attentive during training."

"Does he work miracles?" George asked gruffly. "Your mom is more excited about Gabe being here than I've seen her in a long time."

Bonita heard the worry in her father's voice. Neither one of them wanted Evelyn to experience another disappointment with Jasmine if Gabe didn't succeed.

"I honestly believe that if anyone can get Jasmine to accept the electric wheelchair, it's Gabe."

"I trust you, *mija*. If you say he can do it, then I believe he can."

Her father hugged her before he left the ranch to run into town to pick up some of Evelyn's medicine. Her mother took a regular round of anxiety and pain medicines to keep her as comfortable as possible.

Gabe was standing in the center of the pen with a winded Jasmine standing beside him.

"You see, she's decided that it's better to stand in here with me instead of out there on the track working," Gabe explained. "Doing this with Val a couple of times a week would go a long way. Remember—whoever moves the feet wins. So when you move a horse's feet, you're becoming the leader of the herd. That's how it works. You have to be the lead mare."

Gabe asked Bonita to get her mom's spare electric wheelchair and bring it out to the pen. It was an older model, but they had kept it just in case the newer version needed to be repaired.

Bonita brought the wheelchair down the ramp but left it out of sight. Usually, Jasmine tried to bolt in the opposite direction when she saw the wheelchair.

"Are you ready?"

Gabe had put a rope halter on Jasmine and had her standing next to him on a grassy spot near the driveway.

"Can you get in it and come toward us like your mom would?"

"Okay."

It was disturbing, sitting in her mom's first electric wheelchair. In light of her genetic test that confirmed Bonita carried the familial ALS gene, it wasn't inconceivable that she could one day end up using a similar chair. But regardless of her discomfort, helping Gabe train Jasmine to accept the wheelchair was more important than any negative feelings Bonita was experiencing.

Bonita moved the chair from the hidden position, around the corner and down the driveway toward Gabe and Jasmine. Jasmine, as she always did, tried to get away. Gabe, in his calm and controlled manner, went to work. Instead of trying to get the horse to stop moving, the cowboy made the mare move more. Every time the horse stopped moving the right way, according to Gabe, he took the pressure off her and asked Bonita to stop where she was.

Little by little, repeating the steps, rewarding the horse by allowing her to stop moving when she was unreactive to the wheelchair, Bonita inched closer to the horse.

"I can't believe I'm this close." Bonita stared in amazement at Gabe.

Jasmine was standing next to him, her ears perked forward, ten feet away from the wheelchair.

"Horses work off of pressure. Remember—everything we do is pressure to them. So a look can be pressure, where my body is in relation to their body can be pressure. The way horses learn what we want them to do is by releasing pressure at the right point. That's the trick."

Shaking her head in disbelief, she said, "You are amazing, Gabe."

That brought Gabe's bright blue eyes directly to hers and for the first time since he'd been working, he held her gaze for several seconds. As it always did, that moment of locking gazes with the cowboy struck a chord in her that was foreign. She had never felt before the way she felt when Gabe looked her directly in the eye and held her gaze.

"Well." He almost appeared embarrassed by her praise. "Let's not get ahead of ourselves. We've got to get that chair, and you in it, right up next to her."

"Do we do that today?"

Gabe reached over and rubbed the mare between her ears. The mare lowered her head into a more relaxed position in response to his gentle touch.

"I think we're gonna get it done today, yes."

It took two hours of work—sometimes slow and painstaking—but by the end of the session, Bonita moved the electric wheelchair up to where Jasmine was standing and held out her hand for the horse to smell.

Tears of joy and relief were on her cheeks as she reached into the pocket of her jeans and pulled out a peppermint.

"There you go, sweet girl." Bonita held out the candy in the palm of her hand for the mare to take.

"I think that's enough for today." Gabe didn't seem to be uncomfortable in the face of her tears.

"Thank you, Gabe." She wiped the tears from her face. "You have no idea what this will mean to my mom."

Gabe turned Jasmine loose in the nearby pasture. Bonita stood up, turned toward the large wall of windows from which Evelyn watched the world and looked to see if her mom had born witness to the breakthrough with Jasmine. In the window, she could see her mother. Bonita waved her arms in the air and then blew her mom several kisses.

"I tell you, I'm running a bit late for my next client. I'd like to come by tomorrow, work with Val and then be here when your mom comes down."

"That would mean a lot." Bonita offered him her hand. "Thank you, Gabe."

He looked at her hand kind of strangely, but he took it, and they shook hands. "You can pay me tomorrow," he said as he got into his truck.

They agreed on a time that would work for both of them, and then Gabe was getting ready to pull away. Once again, they locked eyes. Again, the cowboy seemed to want to add something or linger in the moment right before he finally moved on.

It wasn't her imagination—there was a strong connection between herself and the cowboy. Bonita couldn't understand it and she couldn't define it—but she could feel it. And she had a strong sense that Gabe felt it, too. There was something there between them.

As promised, Gabe showed up at the ranch the next day, on time and ready to work. He greeted her with a tip of his hat and a smile in those blue eyes, but he wasn't in the mind-set for too many pleasantries. She knew that he had fit her into his schedule for the day, so it was understandable that he had to focus on the horses.

Gabe made the decision to work with Val first, and

Bonita was sincerely relieved to have someone to talk to about her new horse—someone who might have a solution to some of the problems she was having with the giant Oldenburg.

Using the rope halter, a training halter that worked on pressure points on the horse's nose and behind the ears, Gabe led the Oldenburg out to the round pen. Bonita stood outside, keenly attuned to the man and the horse. Gabe started to put the Oldenburg through his warm-up exercises, asking him to back up and move his front feet and then his back feet.

"I guarantee this horse hasn't had this kind of training," he said. "So it's going to take him a couple of sessions to learn his job. And even then, he's going to need to practice to keep the skills. I can't do it today, but we'll set up some sessions and I'll teach you to do what I'm doing now."

Bonita watched Gabe put the seventeen-hand-tall horse through some sending exercises, where he directed Val from one side of the pen to the next. The idea of having the Oldenburg cantering that close to her while she was on the ground made her feel anxious. It was difficult to imagine that Gabe was ever going to be able to teach her his techniques; they were so foreign to her years of experience.

Gabe removed the rope halter and set the horse's pace, asking Val to walk, trot and canter, first to the right and then to the left, forcing him to go in the opposite direction on command. When the cowboy wanted the horse to slow, he didn't use a voice command. Instead, he used his body, letting out a breath, relaxing his shoulders—subtle changes—and to Bonita's amazement, the horse always slowed. As with Jasmine the day before, Val walked up to Gabe in the center of the round pen and stood quietly with him. After a moment, the cowboy reached over and rewarded the gelding with a rub on the neck.

"All a horse wants is a strong leader and you need to be that leader. Like I said yesterday, you need to be the lead mare. If this horse—or any horse for that matter—feels any weakness in you at all, they are going to try to take the lead position and boss you around. That's their nature. We're asking them to live in our worlds in an unnatural way but we need to understand how they communicate, what their motivation is, if we are going to be safe with them."

Gabe stepped away from Val, and to Bonita's surprise, the Oldenburg began to follow him. If Gabe turned right, Val followed. If he halted, so did the Val.

"You want the horse to look up to you. When the horse is willing to follow you, that means they see you as the leader," Gabe explained while he was walking. "The more you work with him, the more he sees you as a leader, the more cooperative he's going to be."

"I've never seen someone do that with a horse before," Bonita said, doubting that she could ever replicate what Gabe was modeling.

He halted and put the rope halter back on the Oldenburg. "What's he like to ride?"

"Same as he is on the ground. Resistant."

Gabe tossed the lead rope over the horse's neck and left him standing in the center of the round pen.

"Do you want me to hold him?" she asked him.

"Nope," he replied as he came out of the round pen. "He'll stand there."

As was typically the case when it came to horses, the

cowboy was right. Val just stood there quietly, awaiting Gabe's return.

Bonita shook her head at the horse. "Who are you and what have you done with the real Val?"

Gabe returned carrying his Western saddle on his hip and a bridle slung over his shoulder.

"I don't think he's ever had a Western saddle on him before!" Bonita exclaimed anxiously. God only knew how the Oldenburg would react to such a different kind of saddle. She was certain that he had only been broken with English saddles, which were totally different in weight and feel than Western.

Gabe didn't seem concerned. He threw the saddle pad onto Val's back and then swung his weathered, dark brown saddle on top of the pad.

"Horses don't care about the type of saddle," Gabe told her. "To them, it's just different dead cow."

Bonita didn't necessarily like the phraseology the cowboy used, but she got his point.

He moved Val out without the bridle on, with the heavy leather stirrups dangling down. "I like to leave the stirrups down," he told her. "Gets the horses used to not reacting to something bumping them on the side."

As Gabe had predicted, Val didn't care about the type of saddle. In fact, she had to admit that he looked pretty sharp with a Western saddle.

"A Western saddle is going to creak a little bit more than an English one, so I'll let him get used to the sound of it before I get on him."

Val settled down quickly, virtually ignoring the novelty of a type of saddle he'd likely never had on his back before. Gabe put the bridle on him and then led him out of the round pen toward the indoor riding arena.

Why she had doubted Gabe for a second was beyond her, Bonita thought as she followed him into the arena. The man truly was a horse whisperer and she was feeling very grateful for having him as a resource for both of their horses.

"He's impressive." Her father joined her at the side of the arena. "Your mom and I have been watching him from the window."

"He's doing everything I would do in my warm-up for dressage in a Western saddle," she said quietly. She had wrongly assumed that because the man rode Western, he wouldn't know the first thing about how to make a horse supple, or lateral work or collection.

Gabe rode Val over to where they were standing.

"What do you think?" she asked him.

"He needs more work on the lateral. A lot of people think that you walk in a circle and that's working on the lateral. You have to start by pulling his nose all the way back to the tip of your boot, to the right and then to the left. That's a place to start with him. Most horses will bite at your boot." He smiled at Val. "Like he is now. That's just their nature."

"He feels like he's fighting me every step of the way when I ride him."

Gabe gave a little nod. "He doesn't have a great work ethic."

That was not what she wanted to hear. It was like a parent hearing from a teacher that her kid was a low performer or a daydreamer. A $750,000 horse with a bad work ethic was never good news.

The cowboy dismounted and led the horse out of the arena. "I think we'll finish here. There's plenty to work on with him, but we need to get to the next."

"Can you get him in the wash rack at least?" Bonita asked. "He acts like he's never been in one before and I need to be able to rinse him off after I ride him."

Of course, Val walked right into the wash rack like he did it all the time and stood quietly next to Gabe.

"Like this?" Gabe asked her.

"Well." She frowned at the Oldenburg. "He doesn't do it like that for me."

Gabe rinsed off Val, squeegeed off the excess water and then handed the lead rope to her. "Be the head mare."

Gabe wasn't often emotionally touched by the experiences of other people. Perhaps he was jaded, but that's just how he was. But he was touched by what he had managed to accomplish for Evelyn, George and their beautiful daughter, Bonita.

First, he had Bonita go through a practice run with the spare electric wheelchair to make sure that Jasmine was still desensitized to the sound and the motion. When Jasmine did her job, not reacting to the wheelchair motion and letting Bonita move into her space, Gabe was convinced that the Thoroughbred mare was ready for real performance.

"If this works, you have no idea what it will do for my mother," Bonita said quietly as they waited for George to return from the house with Evelyn.

When he didn't know what to say, Gabe just kept quiet. But when it came to how a horse might respond, he could speak his mind just fine. Standing next to her, he could feel the anxiety and worry coming off of Bonita's body like a magnetic field.

"If you're doubting she can do it, you're putting that doubt off on the horse."

Bonita turned her deep, brown eyes up to his—eyes that had been in his dreams of late—took a deep breath in and let it out slowly as she nodded her understanding. He could see how important this was for their family and he felt proud to be a part of a solution.

"Please work," he heard Bonita whisper beside him as her mother and father came into sight.

When Evelyn and George came within earshot, Gabe said to Bonita's mother, "Expect her to succeed. Just come on over like you do it every day."

Gabe had worked at several facilities that used horses for therapeutic riding with individuals with disabilities, so this wasn't his first time training a horse to work with a wheelchair. Bonita hadn't told him the reason Evelyn was confined to a wheelchair, but to him, she was just another client with just another horse.

"Good girl, Jasmine," Evelyn said in her slurred, slow speech.

Instead of backing up or trying to escape Evelyn as she had before, the Thoroughbred stretched her neck forward and smelled her owner's hand. Bonita's mother struggled to lift her hand but managed to touch the soft leather of Jasmine's nose.

George was standing behind his wife and Gabe could see that he was fighting a rush of emotion, while tears freely flowed down his wife's cheeks. Bonita quickly moved to her mother's side, wiped the tears away from her cheeks with her hands and placed a kiss where the tears had just been.

"I have a treat for her," Evelyn said.

"Here, Mom," Bonita was quick to say. "Let me help you."

Bonita found a peppermint, Jasmine's favorite treat,

in her mom's shirt pocket. Evelyn's fingers were curled under from atrophy, so Bonita stretched out the fingers, put the treat in the palm of her mother's hand and let the horse take it.

Gabe watched the family as they accomplished something so seemingly small and yet it was an enormous event for them. Evelyn feeding a treat to Jasmine was a hallmark moment. Bonita was laughing through her tears and George was praising Jasmine, patting her on the neck and laughing. Evelyn was, as much as she could, smiling with her mouth. But mostly, Gabe was touched by the joy he saw in Evelyn's eyes.

George paid him for his work both days plus a hefty tip before he took his wife back to the house. They turned out Jasmine into the pasture and then Gabe was once again alone with the woman who had occupied much of his thoughts for the last week.

There was something about Bonita that he couldn't get off his mind. There was sadness in her he wanted to fix. When he was with her, he didn't want to leave her. And when he wasn't with her, he thought about getting back to her. It had been a long time since he had fallen in love and gotten burned to a crisp. He wasn't completely sure, but what he was feeling for Bonita felt an awful lot like falling in love.

Bonita walked back to him, her eyes red from crying. Normally she shook his hand when they said goodbye, but this time, she forwent the handshake, crossed into his personal space and hugged him. It wasn't a long hug, but it was a hug that had some heart behind it.

Her arms crossed in front of her body, Bonita said to him, "I owe you an apology, Gabe. I do. I had no idea when I met you, that you were the one—"

Bonita's voice caught and he wanted to hug her again. "The one who could give my mom such a beautiful gift." The pretty heiress turned her brown eyes to him and held his gaze. "My family—*I*—am forever grateful."

## *Chapter Nine*

Hugging Gabe seemed as natural as breathing to Bonita. It had happened spontaneously, from the heart, and she meant that hug. Gabe had been stiff and hadn't hugged her back, but she didn't take offense. Gabe was a bit physically standoffish. Her family, especially her father's family, was very touchy-feely and hugged and kissed all the time.

"I know you're running late because of us." Bonita had caught him looking at his watch. "So, again. All I can say is thank you for everything."

Gabe gave her his typical simple nod. "Pleased to have been a help."

They walked together to his truck, but instead of opening the driver's door, he stopped and looked down at her as if he still had something to say. Usually he didn't say a word in that moment, but this time, he did.

"Do you want to come with me?" he asked her. "My next client needs me to get their mule to load in their trailer."

Bonita laughed—somehow, he could always make her laugh. "I have to tell you, that's the strangest offer

I've ever had. Why do they want to get the mule on the trailer?"

"They compete in mule dressage shows."

Now she was laughing even harder. "Mule dressage? Is that real?"

"Apparently it's a thing."

They laughed together for a second or two.

"That's just silly." She smiled at him.

"I don't judge." Gabe smiled back at her. She liked his laugh. She liked his smile. And she liked his clear blue eyes. "I just work through the problem."

"And how could I possibly help you?"

"I was thinking you could get into the trailer and bray while I tried to move his feet."

His suggestion made Bonita laugh again. "Wow. That's quite an offer. I suppose I should find out how much it pays before I turn you down. How much does it pay?"

"Not much."

Their eyes met and held as he continued.

"Now that our business is done for the day, I'd like to talk about that date you promised me."

"A meal between two friends, if I recall the offer." She said with a playful smile.

"I'd still like to take you to dinner. But, I was thinking I would take you out on my boat first."

Bonita wanted to spend time with Gabe, and she knew that her mother would want her to go out and have a good time with him, too.

Evelyn would take joy in Bonita living her life. It was making her mom unhappy that the people she loved had put their lives on hold. As difficult as it was, making some attempt to fill her life with something other than her mother's medical care would contribute to her mom's happiness. But now, with her positive genetic test, Bonita was faced with an odd feeling of obligation to any man who seemed interested in her on a romantic level. When was it appropriate to share that kind of news with someone? After her experience with her longtime boyfriend, now ex-boyfriend, Bonita believed that it was better to scare them off right away rather than allow her heart to get attached to them. Better to be sad now rather than devastated later.

"You never asked, but my mom has ALS," Bonita said. "That's why she's in a wheelchair." Gabe didn't respond, so she clarified, "You may have heard it called Lou Gehrig's disease."

Gabe gave her a nod of understanding. She could see by his expression that he was trying to figure out where she was going with the conversation.

"She has a rare form of ALS. Familial ALS, which means, what's happening to her…" Bonita stopped only because she was having difficulty saying the words out loud to someone she didn't really want to scare away "…could happen to me."

She watched his face very closely, trying to decipher every nuance of his reaction. The truth was, there wasn't much there. He just looked at her like he always did—like he thought she was pretty.

"Do you understand what I'm trying to say?"

"I understood you," he said with a bit of impatience for the question. "You could get sick down the road."

She nodded.

"I suppose I'm more like a horse than a human because I like to deal with right now. Today. I'll deal with the future when it gets here."

That made her smile.

"So can you help me with the mule?" Gabe asked with a glimmer of humor in his eyes.

"I'm afraid I'm going to have to pass on the mule training," she told him. "But I will take you up on that boat ride offer."

Their eyes met and held and Bonita had the strong feeling that Gabe was thinking about kissing her. He didn't, but she could see it in the way his eyes had drifted, ever so briefly, to her lips.

"I'll pick you up," he said, but there was a question for her approval in his eyes.

She nodded. "You'll pick me up."

Bonita watched the cowboy drive away, waving her hand in farewell as he disappeared around a curve. Even after he was out of sight, she didn't move from her spot.

Standing beneath the expansive, blue Montana sky, Bonita felt unburdened and light. It had been a truly magical day, from her mother's success with Jasmine to Gabe not running away from her because of her possible medical future. He was a strong, stable, kindhearted, talented man and he made her want to push aside all of her preconceived notions about Montana men and just look forward to her first real date with a cowboy.

It took Gabe two days to plan for his day trip with Bonita to Canyon Ferry Lake. Now that he was actually going through with a date, something he really hadn't done in a while, he was beginning to understand just how out of practice he was at that sort of thing. He had worked hard to earn the respect he now saw in her eyes when she looked at him and he didn't want to lose the ground he had gained with her. He liked her. He genuinely liked her.

Beyond the occasional casual hookup when he was out of town, Gabe had kept his love life on lockdown in his own backyard. It was bad enough that he had to see his ex, Mandy, in town with her three kids that could have been his and he didn't want to compound that discomfort by adding more women to the list. But there was something about Bonita that had made him break his rule. He hoped he didn't live to regret it.

"I didn't know what I should bring." Bonita had been sitting on top of one of the pasture fences awaiting his arrival. He wanted to leave before sunrise and he expected her to at least lodge a complaint for the early departure.

Wearing a pair of jean shorts and an oversize, long-sleeve T-shirt over her bathing suit with a striped beach bag slung over her shoulder, Bonita hopped down from the fence and walked toward him. He loved how curvy her hips were—she wasn't too skinny. She was toned from years of riding and she had a womanly figure he appreciated.

"Just yourself. I took care of everything else." He opened the passenger door for her.

"Tater!" his date exclaimed when she saw the Chihuahua in her seat. She scooped up the dog, hugged her and kissed her. "I was hoping you were going to bring her."

Maybe Tater was a bit of a crutch for him. The dog had been a valuable buffer during the awkward first day of the trip home from Virginia. Gabe didn't know if this first date would be awkward between them, but just in case, he'd brought an insurance policy in the form of Tater.

Bonita was still fawning over Tater when he started the truck. "We've got about an hour and half trip to the lake."

"I'm excited," she told him. "I haven't been boating in a long time. I love it, though. I looked up Canyon Ferry and it looks incredible."

"I try to get up there at least a couple of times a month to fish."

He didn't tell her that he usually went to the lake alone. Sometimes one of his brothers or a friend would join him, but for the most part, just like hauling horses, going to the lake was something that he typically liked to do alone. And yet, he'd asked Bonita to come with him without giving it a second thought.

"I like your boat. Of course, I'll be able to see it better when the sun comes up."

Gabe looked over at his date and smiled. There it was, pretty much right on schedule—the complaint about the early-morning departure time. "You could close your eyes and catch a quick nap."

"No." She shook her head. "I don't want to miss the trip."

In that moment, it occurred to Gabe that he felt truly happy to have Bonita beside him. He'd missed her company on the road. Even when they weren't talking—when they were just watching the world go by in the quiet—having this woman with him made sense in reality even though they sure as heck didn't make much sense on paper.

Gabe got the boat off the trailer and, using one of the public boat slips at the lake, into the water without much fanfare. While Bonita waited with Tater, Gabe found a place to park his truck and then they were ready to spend the day on the water. From all the weather forecasts she had seen the night before, they were going to have a sunny day ahead.

The boat had three seats at the control cockpit. Bonita sat in the seat on the far end, leaving a space between them. Holding on to Tater, she breathed in the fresh morning air and smiled as Gabe slowly drove the boat away from the shoreline. The first morning light was creating a golden ribbon of light that followed the ridges of the tree-lined hills surrounding the lake and taller mountains far off in the distance. It was early on a Monday morning and they had the lake to themselves. This was the one day they could find when they were both free. After he took them a ways offshore, Gabe shut off the engines in the middle of the lake and dropped anchor.

"This is what I wanted you to see."

Together, in silence, they watched the sun rise. Yes, she had seen a sunrise before, but in this setting, with no other humans in sight and the yellow glow of the sun casting strands of gold and amber and crimson across the green of the trees, it was unlike any she had experienced before. It was magnificent. In Bonita's mind, she had never felt closer to God. Her hand instinctively went to the gold cross that she always wore around her neck and she said a small prayer for her mother and her father.

"I have traveled all over the world," she told Gabe quietly. "Africa, New Zealand, Europe, Egypt. But, in my whole entire life, I have never seen any place more beautiful than right here, right now."

"I don't know why," he said, "but I believed you would understand."

Bonita nodded, not wanting to fill nature's church with too much unnecessary talking. She did understand. This was Gabe's sanctuary and he had wanted to share it with her. It was a moment that they had shared that she would not soon forget.

After the show was over and the sun had settled in the sky, Gabe pulled anchor and took her on a tour of the entire lake.

Her sunglasses on, her hair back in a high ponytail and her favorite three-legged dog in her lap, Bonita felt as light as the wind brushing over her face. She found herself laughing for no reason at all, other than the fact that she felt happy in the moment. Gabe found a tranquil, picturesque spot to drop anchor and he set up the food that he had brought for breakfast. He had gotten freshly baked, giant cinnamon buns, a thermos full of hot coffee, with cream for her, and a couple of dog treats so Tater wouldn't feel left out. Gabe had also thought to bring some fresh fruit to round out the meal.

They sat on the forward deck of the boat on soft cushions, flocks of birds serenading them as they flew overhead. The water on the lake was calm, so the rocking of the boat was gentle and soothing.

It was in these moments that Bonita missed her mom the most. Evelyn had grown up on the water—her father had been a captain in the navy. Boating was in her blood. The fact that she was out here on this incredible lake in Montana, where her mother had always dreamed of living, and Evelyn was stuck back at the ranch confined to a failing body, infused the happiness Bonita was feeling in the moment with a large dose of sadness.

"Where did you go?" Gabe's question interrupted her inward reflection.

She forced a small smile for his benefit but decided to be honest with him. "I was thinking about my mom. She would love this."

"You feel guilty."

She took a sip of warm coffee and then said, "Yes. I suppose I do. This is her dream, not mine. And here I am enjoying it."

He looked off into the distance in thought. "I think we could find a way to get her onto my boat. I'd be happy to take her out on the lake. Anytime."

Bonita put her hand on his arm and squeezed it for the briefest of moments. "Thank you for the offer, Gabe. But I'm afraid my mom has lost her will for adventure. She used to venture farther away from the ranch, even six months ago, but…" her voice trailed off "…the whole reason I'm here today—not just in Montana but here with you—is because of my mom. She wants me to take some time for myself." She caught Gabe's eye. "I think she's preparing me. Weaning me off of her one excursion at a time."

A well of emotion broke through at the thought of the day when her mom would no longer be with her. Bonita turned her head away and rubbed her fingers over her eyes hard to stop the tears from forming.

When she turned back to Gabe, she forced another small laugh and a smile. "I really know how to tank the mood, don't I?"

"You're fine."

"I suppose I don't really have too many people to talk to about it. You don't want to burden your friends every time you speak with them."

Gabe finished off his cup of coffee, seeming unfazed by the topic of her mother's illness. "You can talk to me anytime." He leaned back and stretched out his legs in front of him, crossing them at the ankles. "About anything you want."

"I believe you mean that."

"I do mean it. Wouldn't say it if I didn't." He patted the spot next to him. "Why don't you come over here and join me? Stretch out your legs, drink some more coffee. Enjoy the view."

Mirroring her date, Bonita leaned back as well, their shoulders touching. She studied his profile—the prominent nose that looked like it had been broken at least once, the strong chin and jawline covered with a day's worth of stubble. This was a man a person could lean on.

Other than her father, she wasn't sure she'd ever met a man who made her feel secure in the knowledge that he could handle anything that came his way. Even her father, whom she had always believed to be invincible, was cracking a bit under the pressure of his wife's terminal illness. She had never thought to see any weakness in her father—he had always seemed like the strongest man in the world. Now she knew, even the strongest of men had fault lines. It made her wonder... what were Gabe's?

They spent the better part of the morning on the lake and had the boat back on the trailer and were heading home before the bulk of the visitors to the lake arrived for the day. She still hated getting up before dawn, but she did understand why Gabe planned it that way. The sunrise had been well worth the pain of getting out of bed, dressed and on the road while it was still dark.

"I appreciate you going with me," Gabe said as he opened her door to let her out.

She couldn't remember the last time a man made her feel so feminine and appreciated. Maybe never. The way he spoke to her, the kindness of his words and his actions, and the solidness of his character, were qualities she hadn't expected to find in a cowboy. Her image of a cowboy came from the movies, not from real life, and Gabe had shown her how wrong her judgment had been.

"I hope you enjoyed yourself," he added.

Her stomach was fluttering with the thought that he might try to kiss her. The entire date had been low-pressure. He hadn't tried to invade her space or force physical contact. He just seemed to want her company with no strings attached. Would that change now? And did she want it to change? It wasn't cut-and-dried for her.

"I had the best day I've ever had in Montana." It was the truth and she wanted him to know it.

Gabe set Tater down on the ground and then he fell in beside Bonita as she walked toward the house. At the front door of her family home, he seemed like he wanted to linger with her a moment or two longer. Their eyes met and Bonita was struck by the clearness of his bright blue eyes. Her mother believe that the eyes were the window to the soul—based on what she saw in this man's steady, unwavering gaze, Gabe Brand's soul was filled with goodness.

"Bonita." He said her name with a slight Western twang that made her smile. "I want to spend more time with you."

His words made her smile. But she said, "I never know what my schedule is going to be with Mom. Things can change so suddenly around here."

He didn't move a muscle, but it felt as if he had pulled away from her, so she was quick to add, "But I want to spend more time with you, too, Gabe. As long as you can accept how things are in my life right now..."

In response, he took her hand in his, kissed it and then tipped his hat to her.

"I'll see you on Wednesday."

Gabe had put Val on his regular schedule and planned on working with the Oldenburg every week for the next month.

"See you then."

Gabe whistled for Tater. The Chihuahua raced up to him and he scooped her up.

"Hey!" Bonita called out to him.

He turned to face her.

"How did it go with the mule?"

He smiled. "May Belle the mule. I heard from the owner yesterday. May Belle is loaded and is off to fulfill her mule dressage dreams."

"Good job, cowboy."

He tipped his hat to her once more. With a final wave, she opened the door to the house, dropped her beach bag off at her bedroom and then headed for the great room to find her mom.

"Huh." Bonita didn't find her mother in the great room. Evelyn had developed a schedule for herself, one that seemed to give her some stability, comfort and control over her own destiny. During this time of day, she was in the great room.

"Oh! Bonita! I was just getting ready to call you." Kim was walking quickly through the great room but stopped when she spotted Bonita.

Bonita's mood plummeted and that horrible knot,

the one that felt like it was tearing at her gut, formed in her stomach.

"What's wrong with mom?"

They had an agreement that if an emergency occurred, the nurses would take care of Evelyn first and then inform the family. In her mother's case, those seconds could mean the difference between life and death.

"The pneumonia's back. We've worked the protocol and she hasn't responded. I've called the ambulance. She's going to the hospital."

## Chapter Ten

Bonita had to cancel on Gabe for that Wednesday, and as it turned out with their schedules, he didn't get to see her for nearly two weeks. He'd been half expecting to get a text from her today saying that she had to reschedule once again; he didn't.

As Gabe parked his truck in a spot near the Delafuentes' stable, he had to admit that he was anxious, and a little nervous, to see Bonita again. Perhaps it was old-fashioned to think in these terms, but he had a serious crush on the heiress. The worst part of it all was that he couldn't be sure his feelings were returned. Of course he could tell that she liked him—yet it was difficult to know if he was just a casual distraction. For him, it went deeper than that.

Gabe grabbed his equipment out of his truck and walked into the stable. He spotted Bonita coming out of Jasmine's stall. She was dressed in the same fawn-colored riding breeches and knee-high riding boots as the day when they first met. She seemed lost in thought and didn't seem to notice him.

"You been riding today?"

Startled, Bonita sucked in her breath and slapped her hand over her heart. *"¡Ay Dios mio!"*

"I didn't mean to scare you."

She blew out her breath and then sent him a weak smile. "It's okay. I was…" She waved her hand in the air. "Off on a cloud somewhere."

Upon close inspection, Bonita's face appeared gaunt from stress and her eyes were sunken. Her hair, pulled back in a quick ponytail, looked as if it hadn't been washed in a couple of days and she hadn't put on any makeup.

"You look tired."

As if on cue, Bonita yawned behind her hand. "Exhausted."

"Everything okay? I know your mom was in the hospital for a while there."

She let a breath out and then yawned again. "Mom's home now. She finally responded to the antibiotics and they let her come home. She's feeling so much better that she even came out to see Jasmine yesterday, which spoke volumes to me. But one of the nurses just quit, so I've been filling in for the night shift until we can find a replacement."

"I can see you're beat. I can come back later in the week. Why don't we do this another day, Bonita?"

"No."

He suspected that the word came out more harshly than she intended. He knew how short he could get with folks sometimes when he was tired and at his wit's end, so he didn't pay any attention to her tone.

After a second, Bonita gathered herself and added, "I need a break. And Val really needs this. I feel so guilty about him. He needs so much more than I can give him right now."

If he could take away some of her worry and stress by working with Val, then that's what he wanted to do. Gabe worked the Oldenburg in the round pen first, working on his respect for humans on the ground. Then he threw his saddle on him and began to train him in the indoor riding arena. When Val was supple and flexible and responsive, Gabe rode the gelding over to Bonita and halted.

"Are you too tired to ride him?"

"Too tired?" she asked him as if she hadn't understood the question. "No. I'm going to ride Jasmine when we're done."

Gabe dismounted, checked the girth and then waved his hand to her. "Come on."

"You want me to ride him in that saddle?"

"Why not?"

"I haven't ridden in a Western saddle since I was a kid!"

"If you can ride in an English saddle, you can ride in a Western saddle."

He could see that she didn't want to walk away from the challenge he had just laid at her feet, but he could also see in her eyes that she was nervous of the Oldenburg.

"Come on. Give it a try," he coaxed her. "That saddle won't bite you."

He gave her a leg up and the look on Bonita's face made him smile.

"This feels bizarre! I feel like I'm in a recliner, not a saddle."

Maybe she wasn't used to riding in a Western saddle, but Bonita was an advanced rider. It seemed to take her a couple times around the arena to get accustomed to the feel of the saddle, but once she got it, she began to perform leg yields and half-passes. When she came around to his side of the arena, she was smiling for the first time since he'd arrived.

"I can't believe it! He's doing a fabulous piaffe in this saddle!" she said as she maneuvered the Oldenburg into a highly collected trot.

Bonita seemed to get lost in the moment, riding Val for another thirty minutes while Gabe admired her skill from the sidelines. Now he understood why Bonita's father had bought her such an expensive horse with potential to show in the most advanced dressage competitions. His daughter had the talent to go as far as she wanted in equestrian events.

"That was the best ride I've had on him!" Bonita halted Val a few feet away from where Gabe was standing, loosened the reins and patted the horse affectionately on the neck.

"You look like a real cowgirl up there. Now all you need is some boots and a proper hat."

With a laugh, Bonita dismounted and pulled the reins over Val's head. "Is that your attempt at trying to assimilate me, Gabe?" There was a glow in her cheeks now and the heiress seemed to have caught a second wind of energy after riding Val.

"You're here now. Might as well join us."

"Well." She smiled at him. "I have to admit. I did like riding in that saddle."

While Gabe took his equipment to his truck, Bonita brushed the saddle marks off of the gelding's back and then turned him out in the pasture. She cut a pretty figure walking toward him, the breeches hugging her shapely hips and thighs, her ponytail swinging behind her. He knew he had something to do with putting that smile on her lovely face. If he hadn't accomplished anything else with his day, he was glad he had managed to at least do that.

"My dad said he paid you in advance for the training."

"We're good."

Bonita looked over her shoulder at Val. "I'm telling you—he's a different horse when you're around."

"He just needs someone to work with him regular is all."

She took in a breath through her nose and then sighed. "I know. I just don't have the time, the energy or even the horsemanship skills to work with him. I wish I did, but I don't."

"I take horses for training at my place, so that's an option."

"You do?"

"I take them for a month or two. Give them some concentrated training."

"It's almost summer. Will you be going down to Florida this year?"

He was surprised that she remembered him telling her that on their road trip. Normally, he did spend the summer in Florida. He could make a lot of money and bank it for the winter. He'd been getting calls from his previous clients for months.

"I think I'll be hanging around here this summer."

Did she look happy to hear that news? He couldn't be sure. But either way, she was a big part of the reason he'd decided to change his summer plans. He wanted to have the chance to get to know Bonita and he couldn't get to know her from all the way down in Florida.

"Let me think about it," she said seriously. "I think that would be a really good option."

There was a pause in the conversation and it was the moment Gabe was looking for. When he was there to train the horses, he was on the clock. It was business. But when business was over, he wanted to get more personal with Bonita.

She smiled at him and he could tell that she was about to say goodbye and leave him, so he caught her hand and held on to it. It was a positive sign to him that she didn't pull away.

"Before I go…" he bent his head down closer to her "…my brother Shane, he plays every now and again in Bozeman. Once you get someone to take over the night shift for you, I'd really like for you to come and listen to him play sometime."

"Thank you, Gabe," Bonita said and she let him hold on to the tips of her fingers. "I'd really like that."

For Bonita, it was a month of change. The last episode of pneumonia combined with the trip to the hospital had left Evelyn depleted. She had been at the hospital for two weeks before she was well enough to return home. But, Bonita could tell that this had been a turning point for the worse for her mother.

Her father was traveling more now, with the full support of her mother, so she felt his absence in that *she* was now the backbone of the team that cared for Evelyn. In a manner of speaking, Bonita had become the woman of the house during that month—she was in charge, and she had stepped up to the plate and filled the role. As part of her newfound autonomy at the ranch, she had decided to take Gabe up on his offer to take Val for training. Every day that she didn't have the time, energy or patience to work with the Oldenburg was a day that he lost condition and developed more bad stable habits.

There was some sadness in watching Gabe pull away with Val in the trailer—comingled with a sense of failure—but it was short-lived. Not having the demand of a high-maintenance horse on top of her duties at the ranch was a relief.

There was also turnover in the staff, but Bonita had finally found the right combination of nurses and household staff to keep the main house organized and spotless, just as her mother liked it. She had also got a handle on the maintenance of the property outside, hiring a ranch manager to monitor the fences, the fields and take care of the stable, pole barns and workshops.

She hadn't wanted to come to Montana; however, Montana was the place that had officially, at least in her mind, made a woman out of her. She felt changed—transformed—on the inside. Following her mom's sage advice, Bonita was determined not to spend her time petrified of a genetic ticking time bomb, obsessing over the first sign of a disease that might never come. Bonita intended to live life fearlessly, facing each day as if she would never get the first symptom that could mean that ALS had chosen her as its next victim. It was her mother's own bravery, the way she had fought the disease at every turn, and how she'd had the foresight and selflessness to prepare the ones she loved for her inevitable departure, that had inspired Bonita to *live* her life.

"I'll do that, Dana." Bonita walked quickly into her mother's suite of rooms. "You can take your break now, if you'd like."

Dana was one of the new hires, a certified nursing assistant—she was young, eager, and Evelyn seemed to like her so far. On her way out the door, Dana handed Bonita the comb she was using to untangle Evelyn's long, damp, wavy hair. Her mother had always worn her hair long; no matter how difficult it was to maintain as her mother's illness progressed, Bonita would not hear of anyone cutting it short.

Bonita kissed her mom on the cheek. "Ever since I was a young, I have loved doing your hair."

This was a special time for her, taking care of her mother's hair. After she dried it with the blow drier, Bonita carefully brushed her mom's hair until it was soft and shiny.

*"Mira,"* she told her mom, urging Evelyn to look at herself in the mirror. "It's beautiful."

Over the last month, Evelyn's speech had worsened—it was unintelligible to those who didn't know her. She could barely speak above a whisper. She had been working with a speech-language pathologist for months to learn how to use an eye-operated communication device, and they had banked a dictionary of words in Evelyn's own voice. But her mother had refused to use it. Just as accepting the wheelchair had been an admission of a step down in function, Bonita was sure that transitioning to the communication device was going to be a difficult a transition for her mother.

They went into the great room together. Evelyn still had limited use of her right hand and was able to direct the wheelchair. It was possible that she would lose that small bit of function over the next two months. Bonita pulled a chair next to her and positioned it so she was facing her mother. She took her mother's hand in hers and smiled at her.

"You'll be happy to know that I'm going out with

the cowboy tonight. He's taking me to hear his brother play the guitar. I think he sings, too, but I'm not sure."

"I like him."

"I know you do." Bonita laughed. "So do I."

"I wish I had met him before I was sick."

Bonita squeezed her mother's hand. "Me, too."

"He reminds me of your father."

She couldn't stop the rush of anger she felt when she thought of her dad. He should be here. He shouldn't have returned to work, traveling at least once a week for several days at a time. His place was *here*, with his wife.

Bonita turned her face away from her mother so she couldn't see the anger in her eyes. "I'm sure you miss Dad."

"No."

The strength of that one word brought Bonita's eyes back to her mother's face.

"Don't."

Evelyn's breath was labored and Bonita could see that she had upset her mother unintentionally. Her mother could read her as easily as she could read a children's book and she knew there was tension between father and daughter.

"Don't be angry with him." Her mother gasped on the words. "He's losing his love."

"I know."

*"No."* Her mother struggled to say that word again, more loudly. "You don't know. But I hope one day you will. Let him mourn in his own way, *mija*. He will need you when I'm gone."

When Gabe saw her, he actually whistled his appreciation and it made Bonita feel justified for all of the extra trouble she'd put into the outfit for her first official evening date with him.

"You are the prettiest High Country cowgirl I've ever seen."

Bonita had searched online for the perfect cowgirl boots and cowgirl hat for the date. She wanted to surprise Gabe, and from the pleased look on the cowboy's face, she had succeeded.

"I have to be honest." Bonita stuck out her foot and pulled up the leg of her jeans. "If I had known cowgirl boots came with crystals, I would have come to the dark side years ago."

Gabe offered her his arm, and they walked together to his truck.

"I wasn't sure if I should wear the hat to the bar. It seems like more of an outside thing."

"A cowgirl's got to have her hat to feel fully dressed."

They drove into Bozeman, and she had to admit that there was a lot more activity in the college town on a Friday night than she had imaged. Bozeman was probably the most Eastern-feeling place anywhere in the big sky state. Perhaps it wasn't a fate worse than death to be a temporary, honorary citizen of the town.

Gabe's younger brother, Shane, was performing at the Copper Whiskey Bar in downtown Bozeman. It had occurred to Bonita that, in his way, Gabe was introducing her to at least some of his family. She had butterflies in her stomach at the thought. She'd been a freshman in college the last time she was introduced to someone's family.

The upscale bar was decorated in high-end finishes that Bonita could appreciate. It was a masculine decor, with dark, heavy woods, brass and supple leathers.

Holding her hand, Gabe led her to a reserved, private booth near the small stage. Instead of sitting across from her, Gabe sat next to her in the booth so they would both be able to watch his brother perform. He ordered a local whiskey and she ordered a whiskey punch.

"Here's to Evelyn." He held out his glass to touch hers.

His sweet gesture only reinforced the kindness of the cowboy's heart. She touched her glass to his. "To Evelyn."

Bonita was two drinks in and looking for the appetizers they had ordered to help sop up some of the whiskey sloshing around in her empty stomach when Liam, Gabe's older brother and her veterinarian, arrived at the bar with his wife, Kate.

Liam was a tall, lean man with sandy hair, chiseled features and an easy smile. Kate was a genuine Montana cowgirl—a natural beauty with wispy Farrah Fawcett locks, golden skin and a toned physique. They made a truly handsome couple.

"You don't mind if we join you on your date, do you?" Liam took the seat across from his brother.

"She's going to have to get used to my family sooner or later." Gabe signaled to the waitress to come back to the table to get Liam's and Kate's drink orders.

"This is truly amazing," Kate said with a smile. "We knew that Gabe had women in is life from time to time, but we've never actually seen one in person before. You're like a unicorn, Bonita."

"Lots of women out there?" Bonita pretended to be shocked.

"I'd spend time with a couple of women here and there," Gabe admitted, "but that's not dating."

"Not dating?" Kate laughed. "What do you call it?"

"That's just being friendly," he said, then he put his arm around Bonita's shoulders. "This here is dating."

The four of them talked nonstop while they waited for Shane to arrive. Kate was a businesswoman, a mother, and she was exactly the kind of friend Bonita would like to cultivate while she was in Bozeman. Gabe and Liam mostly talked to each other, catching up, while Bonita and Kate bounced from one subject to another, clicking in a way that let her know that they could easily develop a friendship.

In fact, the two of them hardly came up for air, only pausing in their conversation when Gabe and Liam stood up and greeted their brother Shane.

Shane was unlike either of the brothers. Yes, he shared similar features and all three brothers had the same incredibly bright aqua blue eyes, but that's where the similarity ended. Shane's hair was long and he wore a full beard that needed a good trim. His clothes were rumpled and faded and there was an absent, almost hollow, look in his eyes. Shane was introverted and somber, which was a light-year leap away from the personalities of his two older brothers.

"Nice to meet you." Shane shook her hand, but he didn't linger at the table with his siblings.

Gabe had told her that Shane had been in the army and served several tours in Afghanistan. It was obvious to the casual observer that his service came with a hefty price tag for the young veteran.

Shane sat on a stool with his guitar and introduced himself in a quiet, husky voice.

"I'm going to be working through some original tunes tonight, so I hope you'll enjoy it. I wrote this first song for a buddy of mine. It's called 'A Good Piece of Gear.'"

Bonita found herself completely mesmerized by Shane's singing, as well as the lyrics to his original songs. Halfway through the performance, she reached for Gabe's hand. There was so much raw pain in Shane's voice—in his lyrics—that she could only imagine how difficult it was for Gabe to hear. When the performance was over, Bonita had tears in her eyes and she clapped longer and louder than she had for any live performer in her life. Shane Brand was a star, even if he never left the small circuit in Bozeman, Montana.

At the end of the evening, Gabe drove her home and she couldn't get Shane's performance out of her mind. With her arm hooked in his and as they walked toward the door of her main house, Bonita said, "Your brother is so sad, it breaks my heart."

Gabe put his free hand on her arm and squeezed it. "It breaks my heart, too. I have to believe he'll find his way back to the world one day."

They hadn't reached the door when he stopped walking and turned her in his arms. The moon was almost full and when she looked up into his handsome face, she knew that Gabe wanted to kiss her. He was slow to warm up, but Bonita had a feeling that Gabe was the type of man who knew how to keep the fire burning hot in a relationship for a lifetime.

"My sweet, lovely Bonita."

Gabe took her face in his hands and he kissed her. He lingered on her lips, not rushing the moment. He was gentle but firm, kissing her like he meant it—letting her know that he wanted more but was willing to wait for as long as it took to get there.

Gabe's hands slipped down to her shoulders and then his arms wrapped around her body, pulling her close. She heard a sigh and realized that the sigh had come from her.

## *Chapter Eleven*

It was an unconventional courtship, but it was a courtship that seemed to work for them. Bonita didn't want to be wined and dined—she didn't want to go to the movies. What she really wanted from her time with Gabe was to put aside, for just a couple of hours, the stress and the responsibilities she carried on her shoulders at the family ranch.

For the next month, whenever their schedules aligned, Gabe took her out on the boat and they spent time at Little Sugar Creek, riding on horseback or cooking a meal together. When they did occasionally go into Bozeman and grab something to eat, he always picked up the tab, but her expectations for what a "date" should be had shifted dramatically. Prior to moving to Montana, a time she considered to be her "old life," Bonita had expected fancy restaurants, top tickets to theater productions and weekend excursions to swanky resorts as acceptable dates. Post arrival in Montana, her favorite date was spending time with Gabe and Tater in the tiny cabin the cowboy had built with his own hands.

Had Montana truly changed her, or was this more

like a hostage response and she had temporarily adapted to her environment? Bonita would only be able to know the answer to that question in time.

"He's a different horse here," she said as she pulled two glasses out of the kitchen cabinet. "He's not biting, he's not fighting being saddled. Will he just revert back to his old ways when I eventually bring him back to the ranch?"

Gabe was cutting up some cucumbers for her salad. He was grilling a steak for himself, but he was always respectful of her choice not to eat meat.

"His training should hold steady across settings. You've learned some techniques so you can reinforce his training." He looked up from his task and added, "And I'm always a phone call away." Then he stepped outside to get the steak off the grill.

Bonita put the glasses of water on the small, hand-crafted oak table, the only place to eat in the small cabin. Gabe's place was really just one large room with different living zones. The living room, with a vaulted ceiling to give it the illusion of space, was separated from the sleeping space only by a large two-sided fireplace. Gabe was a minimalist—he didn't want much and he didn't have much.

She liked his cabin, but she also liked her things. It was difficult to imagine what she would have to give up in order to live in such a small space. Was Gabe's preference for a minimalist lifestyle the reason his one and only relationship failed?

They had just had an awkward run-in at the grocery store with his first love and high school sweetheart. Mandy had been with her husband and her three kids. It was hard for Bonita to imagine Gabe, who lived in a tiny cabin and preferred to travel alone, with a wife and a houseful of kids. But the encounter did seem to give Bonita an opening to broach a subject with Gabe that she had been considering bringing up for several weeks.

He came in from outside. "About another fifteen minutes and then we can eat."

She was sitting on the couch in the living room with Tater on her lap. Gabe joined her, and as he liked to do, he lifted her legs and put them over his thighs.

Her heart was beating a bit faster at the thought of bringing up his ex—it was a topic about which he was usually a closed vault. He had mentioned Mandy, said they had broken it off, end of story. But after seeing them together at the grocery store, it was clear that there were years of history and hurt between Gabe and his ex.

"Mandy seemed really nice." It was a trite thing to say, but Bonita didn't really have a better way to start the conversation.

Like a blind closing on a window, the expression on Gabe's face changed at the mention of her name.

"Beautiful boys," she continued in spite of all of the "change the subject" signals she was getting from him.

No response.

"You never did tell me why you broke up."

His features hardened. "The past is the past."

That's what he always said whenever she asked about his previous relationships. "What we learn in the past helps us grow into our future," she countered. "I don't mind telling you why my fiancé and I broke up."

"That's your business."

Bonita rolled her eyes and sighed heavily in frustration. Trying to have a conversation of any depth with Gabe was nearly impossible. Horses, fishing and boats, no problem, he'd talk your ear off—anything else, it was like pulling teeth to get him to talk.

"Do you still love her, is that it?"

A flash of genuine anger penetrated the blank wall he had erected in his eyes. Gabe abruptly stood up, his jaw set.

"Look, if your ex let you go for any reason, then he's a flat-out idiot. If you were mine—*really* mine—I'd hold on tight, you can believe that."

"He couldn't handle my mom's illness or the possibility that the same thing could happen to me. He was scared," Bonita told him. "And I don't blame him for that. Not anymore."

Gabe gave a small shake of his head. "I wouldn't let you go. Not for any reason."

"How can the possibility of what's happening to my mom happening to me not scare the crap out of you?" she asked incredulously. "You've seen her and she's only gotten worse. She's petrified. My dad's petrified. *I'm* petrified! Why aren't you?"

"Because I'm not built that way, Bonita. I'm living for today and that's it. Whatever happens tomorrow, I'll deal with it then."

"Would you deal with it by walking away?"

"I just said that I wouldn't!" Gabe stabbed the palm of his hand with the pointer finger of his other hand. "If you love someone, you never leave them. If you take a vow, you keep it. I do dangerous work for a living—I have a friend, one of the best horse trainers in the business, who's a quadriplegic. She was in a horse trailer at night with a horse she didn't know and the horse spooked and crushed her. If we were married, and that happened to me, would you up and leave me?"

"No," she said. "Of course not."

"Then why would I leave you, if we end up on the wrong side of this thing?" Gabe asked. "Does the thought of that happening to you spook my mule? Hell yes, it does! But I don't live in fear of anything or anybody, Bonita. You aren't going to catch me running scared."

They stared at each other for several long seconds and Bonita saw an opening that she decided to take. Gabe was finally talking and she didn't know if it would happen again anytime soon.

"I saw the two of you together and there seems to be a lot of unfinished business there. Do you still love her?"

He looked up at the sky as if he were seeking help from God to deal with her question. Hands planted on his hips in a frustrated stance, Gabe shook his head again and then said, "I've known her since we were kids. We grew up together. I'll always care about her. But you're a smart woman, Bonita. I just don't get how you don't understand how things are between us. I don't love *her*, I love *you*."

Of all the things he could have said to her, professing his love in that moment hadn't been on her short list. Caught off guard at the sharp turn the conversation just took, Bonita pointed to the door. "I think your steak is burning."

Seeming to be as anxious to escape the conversation as she was, Gabe went outside. He returned a moment later with a charred piece of meat. He threw the smoking steak into the sink and cursed. He stood at the sink for a moment and when he returned to the couch, he seemed calmer.

"She wanted to get married and have a family and I wasn't ready. That's all there is to it. We broke up, I left to train in California, and when I got back, she was engaged. I took another trip and when I got back she was married. Now it seems like she's got another kid every time I get back into town."

"I'm sorry."

"Don't be. I'm not. I wasn't ready for all of that."

"Are you now?"

"With the right woman."

Bonita swallowed hard several times, willing herself to tell Gabe something she had been holding back since their first date on the boat. Back then she hadn't known if it was something that even needed to be discussed. Now it did.

"If you want kids, then I'm definitely not the right woman for you."

Gabe watched her and waited for her to finish.

"Even if I never develop ALS symptoms, I carry the gene. I refuse to pass this horrific disease down to one more generation." Bonita looked him directly in the eyes. "I had my tubes tied last year. I will never bear a child of my own."

"I have seven siblings." That was his unexpected response to her revelation.

Her thought was *so?*

"Six brothers," he added. "I think the Brand legacy is safe."

"You don't care about having your own kids?"

She'd seen an awful lot of Montana men proudly toting around their mini-cowboy sons complete with cowboy boots, cowboy hats and button-down shirts. She'd often imagined a little boy with Gabe's handsome features and his striking eyes, but she had always known that she wouldn't be the woman to give him that little boy.

"I don't care about having kids. I care about having you."

"If that's true, then why have things between us been running on idle for so long, Gabe? I'm trying to figure this out. You won't *talk* to me."

"What the heck do you mean by *running on idle*?" Did she really have to spell this out for him?

"You kiss me but that's about as far as it goes."

Now his expression was registering complete surprise. "Is that what this is all about? I've been trying to go nice and slow for you, Bonita! With all that you've got going on, the last thing you need is some guy pushing up on you! Believe me, woman, I've got other gears."

She locked gazes with the cowboy, wanting to get lost in those aqua blue eyes of his. It took her the span of five heartbeats to say, "I'm ready for a higher gear."

Gabe picked up Tater from Bonita's lap, kissed her on the head and put her down on the ground. "Sorry, Tater. It's my turn now."

His mind had switched from the hunger in his stomach to a new hunger entirely. Not wanting to lose the moment, Gabe picked Bonita up in his arms and carried her around the fireplace to his king-size bed. The fact that she didn't protest and instead placed her hand over his heart only served to embolden him. If Bonita wanted him to love her, he was more than ready, willing and able.

By the bed, he kissed those full, naturally pink lips,

loving the feel of her mouth pressed against his. He was going to kiss this woman all over her body, something he had wanted to do for a long time.

Gabe put Bonita down on the bed gently and then closed the blinds on the large picture window that brought light into the small sleeping space. It was private at Little Sugar Creek, but his brothers were known to stop by unannounced.

Tater used the steps he had built for her to climb up onto the bed to join them.

"No, Tater." Gabe picked her up and put her down on the floor. "Go to your bed."

The Chihuahua complained with a little bark but trotted off toward her overstuffed dog bed in the living room.

Gabe was grateful that he would be making love to Bonita for the first time in the afternoon. Even with the blinds closed in the sleeping area, there was enough light streaming in from the rest of the house for him to see her. He wanted to see her; he'd been dreaming of this moment and he didn't want her beauty to be hidden by the dark.

Wordlessly, Bonita let her hair down from the topknot she had fashioned that day. Her thick, long, flowing hair cascaded down over her shoulders. The days of waiting to bury his face in that hair, to feel the silken strands on his body, were over.

The woman of his dreams watched him unbutton his shirt and pull it out of the waistband of his jeans. He shrugged out of his shirt and tossed it on a nearby chair. He wasn't shy about being naked in front of her—he was scarred and bruised and wiry from years of ranch work and horse training. But he knew he could please her if she would let him. He was worried about his hands; as rough and calloused as they were, he didn't want them to scratch her soft skin.

Gabe didn't take much time to strip down to his boxer briefs, knowing that, like many woman, she might want to get a look at what he was working with in the equipment department. He had already gotten aroused thinking about the lovemaking to come, so Bonita could window-shop while he stood nearly naked in front of her. He had already bared his heart to this woman— getting naked was the easy part.

With an accepting smile in her eyes, Bonita moved to the edge of the bed, knelt on the bed before him, put her hands on his stomach and tilted back her head for a kiss. Gabe took her face in his hands, held her captive and kissed her with the pent-up passion he had been feeling for months.

He possessed her with his lips and his tongue, tasting her, exploring her and letting himself get lost in the warmth of her mouth. He was the one in control of that moment, until he felt her hand move from his stomach to the heavy bulge in his underwear. At the mere touch of her hand, Gabe broke the kiss, closed his eyes tight and rested his forehead against hers. He was going to have to be careful not to lose too much control with this woman—he hadn't prepared for this moment and he could finish way too quickly if he didn't keep a tight rein on his passion.

When he lifted his head and opened his eyes, Bonita was smiling a small, pleased smile. He tugged on her shirt that was tucked in neatly to her slim-fit jeans. She didn't resist when he pulled the garment free from her jeans and moved to lift it over her head and off her

body. She was wearing a delicate satin-and-lace bra in
the lightest of pinks. Her breasts, pushed up a bit by
the bra, were full and rounded and tempting. He ran a
single finger along the line of the lace, leaving a trail
of goose bumps in his wake.

Gabe put his hands on her shoulders, ran them down
her arms. He laced his fingers with hers and coaxed her
to stand before him. He couldn't resist taking her in his
arms, feeling her thinly clad breasts pressed against his
chest while he kissed her.

Her fingers beat him to the button of her jeans and
she was laughing a little as she tried to unzip them and
still keep her lips kissing his. She wiggled out of her
jeans, stepped away from them.

Gabe stepped back and admired her; she was wearing bikini bottom underwear that matched her bra. He
loved the curve of her hips and how muscular her legs
were from years of riding. Her body had changed since
her arrival in Montana—her arms were thicker from the
work in the stable and around the ranch and her waist
had thinned. The lower half of her body was still lus-
cious and toned and rounded, and he appreciated her
womanly figure.

Gabe spun her around so her back was to him, pulled
her back against him, ran his hands slowly over her
breasts and her stomach, down the lacy band of her
underwear while he kissed the back of her neck. Her
breathing became quick and shallow and he was en-
couraged by the little gasp he heard when his fingers
slipped inside of her panties. She was warm and wet,
just for him.

He unhooked her bra and slipped the straps down
her arms. She turned in his arms to face him again. Her

breasts were round and natural and the nipples puckered with the anticipation of his mouth.

"Beautiful," he murmured and bent down to take one of her nipples into his mouth.

Bonita's hands were on his shoulders, her head back, her eyes shut and she moaned in pleasure as he suckled her breast. The ache in his body made him want to strip off her panties and sink into her fast and deep and hard, but he forced himself to slow down. This was his moment to please Bonita—to show her that he could give her body everything it needed. He dropped one last kiss on her taut nipple and then guided her back onto the bed.

"Lay back," he commanded quietly.

There was a question in her eyes, but there was trust as well.

He leaned down, kissed her stomach and then pulled her panties down over her hips, down her thighs and then tossed them away. Bonita's knees were together; he ran his hands up her thighs, her skin so silky to the touch, and then put his hands on either side of her knees.

"You know what I want." His voice had deepened with desire.

Bonita nodded, the lids of her eyes lowered. He was grateful that she allowed him to gently separate her thighs to reveal her sweetest gift. He had wanted the taste of this woman on his lips for such a long time.

Gabe knelt before her, humbled by her beauty, and kissed her. She moaned with pleasure and he deepened the kiss, tasting her, loving her, with his tongue and his lips. This was not something he intended to rush; he wanted to feast on her until she was panting and squirming and crying out his name.

His hands on her breasts and his mouth on her sensitive core, Bonita's thighs tightened on his shoulders and he heard her gasp and begin to shudder and he knew that she had reached a peak. She reached for him, holding on to his hands and arching her back.

"Gabe!" she cried out.

He kept right on kissing her until she was limp and spent and pulling him toward her.

Bonita's eyes had a surprised look in them and she whispered huskily, "What was that?"

He smiled at her. "Me loving you."

For the next part, he wanted Bonita to be warm and comfortable and safe. He pulled back the blanket and sheets. "Get under the covers."

His love obliged him, willing to follow his lead after the pleasure he had just given her. Gabe stripped off his underwear. His erection still hard, sprang free. Bonita's eyes moved down to look at him and he was pleased that she didn't appear to be disappointed with the view. He joined her in his bed and pulled her into his arms.

They were body to body, skin to skin, and they kissed each other breathless. Impatient for more, Bonita tugged him toward her, wanting him on top of her. Gabe rolled away for a moment, opened his drawer and pulled out a condom. Bonita had told him that she couldn't get pregnant, but it was his habit to wear one. She didn't object when he came back to her after he rolled on the condom. She opened her arms to him and made room for him between her thighs.

On top of her, careful not to put too much weight on her, Gabe looked down at her lovely face, inhaled that wonderful lavender scent of her skin and couldn't believe that the dream had become a reality.

"You are so beautiful, Bonita."

She reached up and put her hands on his chest. "You are so handsome, Gabe."

And then he was inside of her. He watched her face as he slid into her, wanting to see her and smell her and feel her all at once. Her eyes drifted closed and she bent her knees to bring him deeper inside. She was so tight and warm and slick that he had to stop, even when he could tell that she wanted him to move, so he could get himself back under control.

He dropped his head down and closed his eyes, concentrating on the feel of her body. He set the pace, slipping in and out of her in long, deep strokes, refusing to give in to her demands to go faster. Gabe wanted to drive her wild—wanted her to want more and more from him. He wanted to prove to Bonita that he was the right man for her, in every way.

When she began to beg him, moaning his name and writhing beneath him, Gabe gave her what she wanted. He pushed deep within her and hit the spot again and again that drove her over the edge. She didn't scream— her face froze in a mask of pleasure and her fingernails dug into his biceps as she trembled in his arms. Just as her peak was ending, Gabe set his own pace, driving into her hard and fast until he found his own powerful release.

## Chapter Twelve

Bonita had only made love to two men prior to Gabe. She had lost her virginity to her high school boyfriend and it had been in the most clichéd of ways: on prom night. It hadn't been an experience that equaled all the hype but it hadn't been *horrible*. Her next lover came during her sophomore year of college, a lover who became her longtime boyfriend and eventual fiancé. Bonita had always thought that the sex with her ex-fiancé was very good. She only had the prom debacle to compare it to, but still she'd always believed that they were above average in that department.

They hadn't been. Lovemaking with Gabe was next generation. She had never experienced an orgasm from oral sex before—her ex wasn't such a fan of that sort of foreplay. It had been incredible, sexy beyond her imagination, and she certainly hoped to experience it again.

"What time is it?" Bonita had fallen asleep in Gabe's arms after they'd made love for a second time. It was dark now, so she had been asleep for several hours, at least.

"I'm not sure," he said groggily.

Bonita slipped out of bed, felt around on the ground for her jeans and pulled her phone out of the back pocket. She winced when the light on her phone came on, temporarily blinding her. Slowly, she opened her eyes and squinted at the screen.

"It's eight thirty!"

Shocked at the time, Bonita noticed that she'd missed ten calls. She sat down on the edge of the bed.

"Oh, no! *Why* didn't I hear the phone ring?"

And then it hit her—she forgot to turn the volume back up after they'd left her mom's morning doctor appointment.

"Oh, no." Her heart started pounding as she pushed the play button on the first message from her mother's nurse.

"Everything okay?"

Bonita didn't answer Gabe—she was too focused on the message. She didn't listen to the entire message— she didn't need to.

"Please turn on the light! I need to get dressed!"

He switched on a lamp next to the bed, sat up and watched her scramble to get dressed. "What's going on?"

"I forgot to turn the stupid volume up on my phone! My mom is in the hospital."

Gabe threw off the covers and started to get dressed. He was finished before she was and she heard him take Tater outside.

She yanked on her socks and then her boots, and then she ran into the living room to find her purse. She was searching for her keys when Gabe brought Tater back inside.

"I'll drive you," he said as he put some food down for the dog.

"No." Bonita found her keys and slung her purse over her shoulder. "I can do it."

Gabe put steadying hands on her shoulders. "It's dark. I know the roads."

He made sense, so she agreed. She felt shaky and her adrenaline was pumping, so perhaps getting behind the wheel wasn't the best idea anyway. While Gabe drove, she made phone calls. She got in touch with the nurse, who confirmed that her mother had been admitted to the emergency room with pneumonia, something she had been battling off and on for months. Then she called her father, who was already on his way back to Montana on his private jet. She was about to dial her aunt Betty's number when her aunt called her.

"Hi, Aunt Betty."

"She's back in the hospital?" Betty asked anxiously.

Aunt Betty was Evelyn's only sibling and they were extremely close. Betty had planned to visit Evelyn the following month, but Bonita had a strong feeling that the visit was going to have to be moved up.

"Yes," she confirmed. "I'm almost there."

"Oh, Bonita. She's told me that she did not want to go back to the hospital again."

"I know, but what is the alternative? She has pneumonia and the antibiotics we have at home aren't strong enough."

"If they put her in intensive care again, they are going to want to put her on a ventilator. Evelyn does *not* want that."

"Okay. Aunt Betty—I'm just arriving. As soon as I have an update, I'll call you."

Gabe stopped his truck in front of the emergency room entrance. She jumped out of the truck. "Thank you, Gabe. I'll have someone take me back to your place to get my car. I'll text you later!"

Bonita raced into the emergency room and was escorted back to her mother's room. Evelyn had a breathing mask on, she was already receiving several intravenous liquids, and she looked so shrunken and frail in the hospital bed that it made Bonita suck in her breath.

Kim saw her and gestured for her to go back out into the hall. Once outside, the nurse closed the door to the room. "She has a kidney infection, a liver infection and pneumonia."

Bonita put her hand over her mouth while she listened.

"They have her on the strongest antibiotics available but she can't have her pain medication or her anxiety medication while she's on it."

"That's not going to work." The anxiety medication was one of the tools Evelyn was using to keep her calm in the face of her declining condition and impeding death. She *had* to have it.

"Her oxygen levels are very low," Kim continued. "They want to put her in ICU and ventilate her."

"She won't allow that."

"If she doesn't, it's time to get hospice involved."

The nurse was only speaking aloud Bonita's own thoughts.

"Is she conscious?"

"On and off. The pneumonia and lack of oxygen are making her foggy, but she knows she's in the hospital and she's not happy about it. I didn't have a choice. She was in medical distress and I had to act."

Bonita put her hand on the nurse's shoulder. "You did the right thing. I'm going to go in and see her."

She went to her mother's side and took her mother's limp hand in hers. "Mom. It's Bonita. I'm here."

She kept rubbing her mom's hand and arm, trying to elicit a response. Finally, Evelyn opened her eyes and looked up at her. Bonita could see that her mother was trying to say something behind the mask.

Bonita removed it and leaned down to hear what her mom was trying to say. In a slurred whisper, she was able to understand what her mother said.

"Take me home."

Tears finally formed in Bonita's eyes. Up to that point, she had been in crisis mode. "Mom. If I take you home, you will die."

Her mom stared at her.

"Take me home."

Bonita had stepped out of her mother's room only long enough to call her father. She was hoping that George would get on the phone and convince Evelyn to stay in the hospital, but when her father had to remind her that it was her mother's life and her decision to make, Bonita knew that she had lost this battle. After a quick trip to a nearby restroom to wipe the tears from her face, Bonita sat by her mother's side until the doctor returned and the discharge procedures could be started.

"I need to get some fresh air," she told Kim. "I'll be back in a minute."

Arms crossed in front of her body, Bonita walked down the corridor to the exit door that led to the waiting area. She pushed the button on the wall to open the door and then walked through, her mind whirling with thoughts.

"Bonita."

Not expecting to hear her name called, her head popped up and she looked around. Gabe was sitting on the other side of the waiting area. He stood up and walked toward her.

"What are you still doing here? Have you been here the whole time?"

He nodded.

"You didn't have to do that."

"I wanted to make sure you were okay."

He fell in beside her and they walked outside. She took in a deep breath of cool Montana air. One thing she liked about big sky country was the air—it was so clean and fresh, nothing like the stale air in the city.

She walked along a sidewalk, wanting to clear her mind a bit while they awaited discharge and transport to the ambulance. Under a lamp, Bonita stopped and stared out at the parking lot. Gabe stood beside her, not touching her and not speaking.

"I'm taking my mom home to die."

Wordlessly, Gabe folded her into his arms and she didn't resist. She needed the comfort. She needed the shoulder to lean on. She wrapped her arms around his waist tightly while tears streamed from her eyes onto his shirt. He swayed with her, side to side, and kissed the top of her head. It was the exact moment she needed to dump the emotion before going back to her mother's room. Her mother didn't need her tears right now—she needed her strength.

"You shouldn't have stayed." Bonita wiped the tears

out of her eyes and off her cheeks. "But I'm glad you did."

They parted ways at the emergency room entrance. She wanted Gabe to go home and get something to eat. They had forgone food for lovemaking; now they were both starving.

"I'll get someone to bring me over to your place to pick up my car."

"I'm booked all day tomorrow. But if you wait, I'll pick you up on my way home and take you there myself."

She nodded. "I'll see you tomorrow."

Gabe leaned down and pressed the softest of kisses on her lips. "If you need me, for anything, I'm only a phone call away."

An odd calm came over Bonita when they had her mother settled back into her own bed at the ranch. Evelyn agreed to have oxygen at home, which would make her more comfortable. Kim worked late to help get her situated and then Bonita insisted that she go home. Her mother fell asleep quickly, an odd occurrence.

"I'm going to the kitchen. I'll be back soon," she told the night nurse. "Call me if there's any change."

Feeling like she was sleepwalking, Bonita made her way down to the kitchen and rummaged through the refrigerator. She managed to find some leftover pasta with marinara sauce and didn't even bother to heat it in the microwave. She took the container, a fork and a peach wine cooler over to the table in the breakfast nook, not bothering to turn on the light over the table. She wanted the light to be dim—it matched her mood.

Just as she was finishing the pasta, car lights shone

in the driveway. Bonita swallowed down the last couple drops of the wine cooler, dropped the empty container and dirty fork in the sink and then went to the
front door. Her arms crossed loosely in front of her,
she walked down the steps of the front stoop toward
her father's car. George was taking his travel suitcase
out of the trunk.

"Hi, Dad."

George shut the trunk, put his burly arm around her
shoulder and kissed her on the top of her head.

*"Lo siento, mija."* He told her he was sorry. "I should
have been here."

She was too tired and too drained to agree with him.
He should have been here. She disagreed with her parents' "end of life" plan for their marriage. Bonita needed
to escape, too, but she didn't go back to DC to do it.

"I've canceled my trips," George told her as they
walked toward the house. "Indefinitely."

"That's good, Dad."

It was the right thing to do.

"How's Mom?"

Bonita had to swallow several times just to get the
words out of her mouth. "We'll call hospice tomorrow."

George didn't respond.

"I think we should send your plane to go pick up
Aunt Betty," Bonita went on. "If she waits until next
month, it might be too late."

"I'll make the arrangements." Inside the house, her father paused and put his hand on her shoulder. "Bonita—
I'm very proud of you. You have always been a blessing
to me and your mother."

She hugged her father, momentarily transported to
a time when her father was the strongest man in the

world and nothing could ever harm her. "I'm glad you're home, Dad. Mom misses you. I know this whole 'give George something to do' was her idea. But it hasn't been working for her. Not really."

"It hasn't been working for me either," her father admitted. "No matter how hard I try to forget, what is happening to my sweet Evelyn is always with me."

Much of the anger and resentment she had been harboring for her father slipped away in that moment. They were all just trying to handle a horrible situation the best way they could.

"I'm going to sleep in Mom's room tonight. I had them set up a cot for me."

"No, *mija*," George said. "I'll stay with my wife tonight. Go get some rest."

The bricks she had been lugging around with her all day were lifted off her shoulder, and the relief couldn't have come quick enough. Bonita climbed the stairs up to her bedroom, each foot feeling as if it weighed one hundred pounds. She didn't brush her teeth or wash her face. She locked the door to her bedroom, stripped off her clothing and climbed under her sheets. In the dark, with the sound of an owl hooting somewhere outside of her window, Bonita cried into her pillow until she fell into a restless sleep.

It had been a long day and Bonita was glad to see Gabe at the end of it. He had picked her up on his way home from a day of training, and he took her back to Little Sugar Creek.

She didn't want to talk about her day—about the meeting with hospice or the decisions that were made. Instead, she wanted to spend time with Val, grooming him and working with him in the round pen. She had learned so much from Gabe about horsemanship and about riding a horse from the ground that she felt she would never approach horse ownership the same way ever again. After she spent an hour with Val, she felt better. Horses were therapeutic; Val had buoyed her spirits.

"We still have the salad from yesterday." Gabe had offered to scrounge up some food for them to eat.

"I'm not all that hungry. But you go ahead."

He threw a sandwich together and joined her on the couch. "You sure you don't want anything?"

She nodded, enjoying the time she was spending with Tater. What she really liked about Little Sugar Creek was the simplicity of the life Gabe had built for himself. It was stripped back and easy, so different from her family's ranch. Even under the best of circumstances, the upkeep and maintenance of the thousands of acres and five thousand square feet of living space in the main house would be a full-time job to coordinate. The ranch had been her mother's dream—what would happen to it when she was gone?

Bonita yawned loudly, covering her mouth with her hand. "I'm sorry. I didn't sleep well last night."

"I'm surprised you got any sleep at all."

Another nod.

"Why don't you lie down for a while? It's quiet here. I'll wake you in an hour or two."

One of the things her mom had taught her over the last few months was to invest in herself, to take care of herself. Before, in her old life, she would have pushed through, acting like superwoman and running her body down until she got sick. Now she understood that she had to matter.

"Do you want to join me?" she asked. It would be nice to have Gabe's warm body next to hers while she dozed off.

He gave her one of his T-shirts to put on and it came down to her mid-thigh. She left her panties on but discarded the rest of her clothing. She got into bed with a happy sigh while Gabe closed the blinds throughout the house.

"How's the temperature for you?" he asked, and she could hear that he was taking his clothing off.

"Perfect."

Gabe joined her in bed; she could feel that he still had on his boxer briefs, which let her know that he understood that this wasn't about making love. This was about her getting rest. The cowboy put his arm around her, taking one of her hands in his hand.

"We are an odd couple," she said quietly.

"What makes you say that?"

"We're so different."

"In some ways."

She laughed. "In most ways."

He lifted his head to look at her face. "But not the ways that really count."

She squeezed his hand hoping to reassure him. "It's not a bad thing. At least I don't think it is now."

Bonita turned onto her back so she could look into his face.

"When we first met, I think I was afraid of starting a relationship with you because of how different we are. I thought that I needed a certain type of man to be happy. But then I started thinking about my parents' relationship. They have been happily married for thirty years and they couldn't be more different. They grew up in different countries, they spoke different languages when they were growing up—Mom is from a blue-blooded Boston family and Dad was raised in a poor family from Mexico City."

She threaded her fingers through Gabe's. "But they met and they fell in love and I've never seen two people more devoted."

Bonita turned her body toward the cowboy and put her hand on his heart.

"Do you know that my grandfather, my mother's father, didn't even come to the wedding? He refused to walk his firstborn daughter down the aisle because my father was Mexican. But when I was born, my grandfather saw a picture of me…" Bonita smiled up at Gabe "…fell in love…"

"Understandable."

"…and he reconciled with my mother so he could get to know his granddaughter."

Gabe kissed her hand and put it back over his heart.

She caught his eye and held it. "I didn't…say anything when you told me you loved me yesterday."

"It's okay." He seemed to want to absolve her of any guilt.

"My mom told me recently to never be afraid to live my truth. She wasn't afraid to live her truth when she married my dad over her family's objections. I think that…maybe… I've been afraid of my feelings for you."

Her hand still on his heart, Bonita continued, "My truth is that I love you, Gabe. I love you."

## Chapter Thirteen

Bonita awakened from her much-needed nap to discover that she was alone in bed. She turned over on her side, hugged the pillow and thought about trying to go back to sleep. Noises drifting in from the kitchen caught her attention and made her decide it was time to get up and face the rest of her day.

"Hi," she said to Gabe, who was standing at the sink, his back to her.

He turned at the sound of her voice and smiled when he saw her. There was always appreciation in his eyes when he looked at her. The man thought she was beautiful and was never shy about letting her know.

"How'd you sleep?"

He was shirtless and barefoot, wearing only a faded pair of jeans that were threadbare and white at the knees and around the pockets. There was something inherently sexy about this cowboy; he was lean, almost wiry, without an ounce of fat on his body. Every toned muscle was easy to see from his biceps to his chest to his stomach. The man certainly ate well, but he burned off a ton of calories with his work with horses and on the ranch.

Her ex had been in good shape—always at the gym—but it was different with Gabe. His body was hard from physical labor. His hands were rough and he carried the scars of years of working dangerous jobs in harsh conditions. He'd grown up in this part of the country, had worked the land since he was a kid, and Bonita had grown to appreciate his kind of raw attractiveness.

"Like a rock," she said.

They met in the middle and wrapped their arms around each other. Gabe rested his chin on the top of her head and she sighed at the feeling of the warm skin of his chest on her face.

"I was going to go outside and get some work done, but I wanted to be here when you woke up."

"I'm glad you did."

They hugged each other in silence for several minutes, and even though Gabe didn't try to change the mood of the hug, his body had other ideas.

Bonita tilted her head back so she could look up into his face; he rewarded her effort with a kiss. She stepped out of the hug, took his hand in hers and led him back to the bedroom. She knew what his body was craving because her body was craving it, too.

Bonita sat down on the edge of the bed, unzipped Gabe's jeans and pushed them down his hips. He laughed at her forwardness, stripping his jeans off the rest of the way and tossing them aside. He left on his underwear, perhaps sensing that she wanted to unwrap her own present. She placed her hand over the outline of his erection, smiling a small, pleased smile at his quick intake of breath. She hooked her fingers onto the waistband of his boxer briefs and slowly, deliberately teased them down until his hard-on sprang free.

Not waiting for him to discard the boxer briefs, Bonita took him into her mouth. Gabe put his hands on her shoulders and groaned. As he had with her, she wanted to drive him a little crazy, but not to the point that they couldn't continue to other positions.

"Bonita." He said her name in a raspy, urgent voice. "That feels too good."

Gabe stepped away from her only long enough to yank off his underwear off and pull his T-shirt off her body, exposing her naked breasts.

"God." He laid her down on the bed. "You're so beautiful."

He began to kiss his way down her body, starting with her lips and her neck. He suckled at her breasts while his hand slipped inside her panties to ensure that she was hot and wet and ready for him. She had revved him into high gear and she loved it.

She helped Gabe push her panties down her thighs and out of his way so he could continue his trail of kisses south. The moment his lips touched her, she gasped. She couldn't help herself. It was a bolt of sensations hitting her at once, making her arch her back and clutch the fabric of the blanket in her fists.

But he was impatient for her this time and she didn't mind. She was impatient, too. He quickly put on a condom and met her under the covers. There was no more foreplay, no fanfare—with one arm bracing himself above her, his eyes on her face, Gabe reached between them and guided himself to her slick opening.

And then he was deep inside her; Bonita closed her eyes and sighed with pleasure. She reached for him, pulling him forward so his weight was on her. He was intense with his lovemaking—different than before.

Every stroke—every kiss—every touch of his fingers on her skin said *I love you*.

That was when she let herself go—let herself relax into his arms and let him take her on the most sensual ride of her life. The first orgasm came so quickly that it caught her off guard, and then a second, more forceful climax followed, driving her fingernails into his flesh. She could feel his muscles tensing and the change in his breathing as he built to his own climax.

Bonita did something she'd never done before—she opened her eyes to watch Gabe. There was sweat on his brow and his features were tense—his eyes were closed. He was so handsome to her in that moment. Her eyes still open, he hit a spot deep within her that made her orgasm in a completely different way—she couldn't stop herself from crying out in surprise.

Gabe opened his eyes and planted himself deep within her. As her last wave ebbed and she felt spent and weak in his arms, he threw back his head and growled in the back of his throat as he finished.

Her lover rested on his forearms while he kissed her forehead and her eyes and her cheeks and finally her lips.

Bonita looked up at Gabe and wiped the sweat from his forehead. "I didn't expect you."

He captured her in the lovely depths of those aqua blue eyes as he said, "I didn't expect you either."

The last month of her mother's life was a celebration. Aunt Betty arrived and the mood of the house shifted dramatically. A near carbon copy of Evelyn, Betty was bursting with energy, goodwill and wine.

"She's not dead yet!" Betty complained immediately

about the somber pall that hung over the ranch. "Quit acting like she is!"

Betty had brought her collection of jazz music and filled her mother's suite of rooms with lively music. Windows were thrown open to let in the light and fresh air, and Bonita could hear her aunt's laughter from just about anywhere in the house. They had gotten her mom out of bed several times to go down to see Jasmine. Thanks to Gabe, the horse still ignored the wheelchair and paid attention to the bucket of carrots in Evelyn's lap.

It took a visit from her over-the-top aunt to snap Bonita out of her funk. Aunt Betty was right—her mom *was* still alive. She had been so focused on making sure prescriptions were filled and equipment was serviced and employee schedules ran smoothly that she had forgotten to enjoy the last moments of her mother's life.

With her father's help, Betty arranged for friends to be flown in from all over the world to visit Evelyn. Evelyn didn't have the strength for long visits, so they rotated people in short, laughter-filled bursts. Evelyn had been dedicated to charity initiatives to support education and reading and fighting poverty. She'd been a competitive equestrian and loved to dance—Betty wanted all of those things highlighted.

Perhaps it was the energy brought into the house by all of Evelyn's friends, but her mother lived much longer than anyone had predicted. It seemed that she was holding on until the last of her friends had arrived. After the last group of friends came to the ranch for a visit, it was as if the store of energy—the doctors called it the "last hurrah"—ran out. Evelyn fell asleep for three days.

"Can it be considered sleep if it lasts for three days?" Bonita asked the hospice nurse.

She only left her mother's side for quick bathroom breaks. She had the nurses bring meals to her so she could be with her mother every second of the last moments of her life. And then, as if out of nowhere, Evelyn opened her eyes the morning of the fourth day.

"Mama." Bonita had tears in her eyes as she leaned over so her mother could see her face. She kissed her mom's cheek and hand and then called for her father, who had been holding vigil with her.

George raced to the other side of the bed. He kissed his wife and pressed his cheek to hers as tears streamed out of his eyes. It was the second time in her life she had seen her father cry.

*"Te amo, mi amor."* Her father told Evelyn that he loved her and called her his love. *"Te amo."*

It was as if she had wanted to hear that he loved her, just one more time, before she closed her eyes and drifted back into that coma-like sleep. Bonita crumpled forward, buried her face into her mother's neck and cried tears of sorrow. It would be the last time she saw her mother's eyes.

Two days later, the hospice nurses continued to administer medicine to make Evelyn more comfortable, but no one expected her to awaken again. Her breathing was so shallow and labored that it was difficult to imagine she was getting any oxygen at all.

"She can still hear you." The hospice nurse put a hand on Bonita's shoulder. "Hearing is the last sense to go."

George and Betty had left the suite of rooms for a

moment, and finally the nurses did as well. In a rare stretch of time, it was Bonita alone with her mother.

"I'm going to read to you, Mom." Bonita opened Kahlil Gibran's *The Prophet* to the chapter on love and began to read the words aloud. It was one of her mother's favorite books, and when Bonita was a teenager, Evelyn had given her a copy to read.

Bonita's voice was choked with emotion as she read some of her mother's favorite passages. Teardrops fell on the pages, and Bonita didn't bother to brush them away. Then she felt something—sensed something—different.

She closed the book and turned to her mother. She lowered her head in sorrow, pressed her forehead into the mattress and took her mother's hand and rubbed it over her hair, trying to re-create what her mother used to do ever since she was a little girl.

She covered her mother's body with her own, hugging her frail shoulders. "Don't leave me, Mom. Please don't leave me." It was a plea that Bonita knew would go unanswered. No matter how hard she held on to her mother, it was her time to rejoice with her Maker.

"I love you, Mom. I love you so much." Bonita's tears soaked the front of her mother's nightgown. And as she said those words, her body exploded all over with a tingling sensation and chills. Bonita sat upright and stared at her mother's face, and knew that it was over.

Evelyn was gone.

Life didn't slow down after Evelyn passed away—in fact, for Bonita, things seemed to speed up.

There were obituaries to write and funeral arrangements to solidify. Evelyn had wanted to be buried in

Montana instead of in the family plot in Boston, which caused an uproar with her side of the family. But George and Bonita planned to carry out her mother's wishes. They did arrange for a service in Boston to be held for family and friends who couldn't travel to Montana for the service. There was equipment to return to companies, final payment to be made for the nurses and CNAs. There was such a flurry of activity leading up to the actual funeral that Bonita didn't have time to really mourn the loss of her mother. She had to switch into business mode and get things done.

Gabe accompanied her to the funeral, and upon her request, his brother Shane played *Amazing Grace*, her mother's favorite hymn. It was a haunting, emotional rendition that had everyone in the church in tears.

But after the funeral was over and her mother had been laid to rest, that was when the weight of her mother's loss began to hit. Betty went home, everyone who had been part of her mother's health-care team had found new work, and her mother's suite of rooms had been cleared of all the medical equipment. It was just her father and Bonita rattling around in that giant ranch house, with one geriatric Thoroughbred out in the barn.

That was when Bonita finally understood why her mother had sent her father on business trips toward the end of her illness—watching a depressed, emotionally lost George drifting around the house was too much. It only took Bonita a week to send him back to the business world where he could be productive and find a way to live his live without his love, Evelyn.

Once George was gone, Bonita closed all of the blinds throughout the entire house, making it dark inside even when it was noon. She only left the house to care for Jasmine and the rest of the time she spent under the covers in her bed.

Bonita was well aware that this was not what her mother would have wanted for her, but in the moment, it was her only way to cope.

Gabe didn't see Bonita much during the month leading up to her mother's death. He didn't take offense to it—he understood. He kept himself busy with his clients and with Val. He wanted the Oldenburg to be have all of his kinks worked out by the time Bonita was ready to have him back at the ranch. And in a way, working with the Oldenburg kept him connected to the woman he loved. Even when he couldn't be by her side, he was working on her behalf.

After the funeral, he had expected Bonita to start coming around. He knew she would be sad—that was to be expected—but he hadn't expected her to fall off the radar. She wasn't answering her phone, his texts, his emails or answering the door when he went to her house to check on her. This had been going on for weeks and he was thinking of ways to get in touch with her father through his brother Liam, who surely had the man's phone number, when Gabe's phone rang.

"Gabe? This is George. Delafuente. Bonita's father."

"Yes, sir," Gabe said, relieved. "I was just about to track you down."

"I haven't been able to get in touch with my daughter. I'm here in DC. I can get there by tonight, but I'm worried about her. Would you go over to the ranch and check on her?"

"That's just it. I have gone over there. She doesn't answer the door."

George told him the keyless code to the back door of the house and the code to the alarm. Bonita didn't have a gun, so he didn't have to worry about her accidentally shooting him.

Gabe didn't wait to get on the road. He headed straight to the Delafuentes' ranch to find Bonita. It was a sprawling house, and Gabe had only been up to the great room, but George told him where to find Bonita's room. Once inside the house, he followed the directions to her bedroom.

The door was shut. Gabe knocked. "Bonita?"

He knocked two more times and then opened the door. The room was dark and a little musty, as if the air hadn't been circulated for weeks. He could see the outline of Bonita's body under the covers, but she didn't move when he called out her name.

He opened the blinds to let in the late-afternoon light.

"Leave those shut!" Bonita's head popped up off the pillow. Her hair was a tangled mess around her face and she was blinking her eyes and frowning severely at him.

"Heck no." Gabe opened the next set of blinds. "It's time for you to cowgirl up and get out of that bed."

"I'm not a cowgirl." Bonita pulled the covers over her head in an attempt to avoid the inevitable confrontation.

He unceremoniously yanked the covers off her body. "Sure you are. You just don't know it yet."

His love turned over, curled up into a ball and tried to ignore him. He reached over, scooped her up and put her down on the ground, forcing her to stand.

"I'm in mourning!" she yelled at him.

"Mourn while you're standing up, Bonita," he said

calmly but firmly. "And we need to get you cleaned up quick because you are *ripe*."

He marched her into the bathroom and guarded the exit while she stripped out of her silk pajamas with food stains on the front.

"Your dad is worried about you."

"I'm fine," she grumbled. "Why can't everyone just leave me alone?"

"Because we love you."

Gabe called George while Bonita took a shower, reassuring him that his daughter was alive and well and he'd have her call later. When he heard the water turn off, Gabe went back into the bathroom and greeted Bonita at the entrance of the shower with a towel. She scowled at him, but she stepped into the towel and wrapped it around her body.

Gabe looked around and saw a chair in front of a vanity.

"Sit right there and I'll brush out your hair for you," he offered.

Bonita sat down heavily on the chair, her face unsmiling as she looked at her own image in the mirror.

He looked around on the counter and found a brush and a bottle of spray-in conditioner.

"Have you done this before?" she asked, her voice raspier than normal.

"What? Brushed a woman's hair?"

She nodded.

"No," he admitted. "But I've brushed plenty of horses' tails and I figure it's pretty much the same thing."

As it turned out, it was pretty much the same thing. He started at the bottom of her waist-length hair and moved upward, section by section, until all the tangles were out and he could comb through the length of it easily. Bonita didn't thank him for brushing her hair; he didn't take offense. She wanted to be left alone and he was denying her.

"Jasmine needs some TLC." He leaned on her bedroom doorjamb.

Bonita looked up at him then and he saw the raw guilt on her face. He had learned one thing about her: she was an animal lover. If she thought her actions were causing even the slightest problem for an animal, it upset her terribly.

Bonita pulled on a pair of jeans, her work cowgirl boots and a plain T-shirt, which she wore untucked.

"I'm ready."

They went down to the stable and he could tell by the look on her face that she was seeing the disarray of the place as if for the first time. The ranch manager was called out of town on a family emergency and she hadn't wanted to be bothered with training a temporary replacement. In her mourning, she had been able to ignore the mess. There were buckets that needed to be cleaned, the aisle was littered with hay and dirt, and Bonita had been moving Jasmine from one stall to the next instead of mucking the stall out. There was plenty of work to be done, and Gabe was convinced that having her get the blood flowing and cleaning the stable for the benefit of Jasmine would do his love a world of good.

Bonita started on the buckets and he started on the stalls. It took them an hour to get the stable straightened around, but by the time they were done, there was some color in her cheeks and some life in her pretty brown eyes.

"I'll go get Jasmine," she told him.

She grabbed the mare's halter and lead rope and walked to the pasture where they'd put her while they cleaned. He watched as Bonita stood at the gate, whistled and called the mare's name. It was dinnertime, so the Thoroughbred willingly came running up to the gate from the far end of the pasture.

After Bonita led the mare into the stable, Gabe picked out the Thoroughbred's hooves and then they put her into her clean stall. He could plainly see that Bonita's spirits were lifted knowing that Jasmine was comfortable. They fed her some grain, put enough hay in the stall to get her through the night, and then Bonita lingered in the stall.

"Good night, my sweet baby." She wrapped her arms around the mare's neck and hugged tightly. "I'm sorry I haven't groomed you or ridden you. I promise to do better tomorrow."

Together, with Gabe's arm draped over her shoulders, they turned off the lights and walked out of the barn into the cool, summer night air. It had turned dark while they had worked and in the sky, there was a round, glowing, full, yellow moon.

"Oh." Bonita stopped and stared up at it. "Mom would love to see this moon."

There was a moment of silence between them—a reverent moment with Evelyn in their thoughts.

"What would your mom say to you if she were here now?" he asked her quietly.

His love breathed in deeply and then let the air out on a long sigh. "She would say get on with it already, Bonita. Go live your life."

## Chapter Fourteen

Gabe's visit had snapped Bonita out of her funk and she was grateful for it. It didn't diminish the pain of the loss of her mother, which felt like a gaping wound that would never truly heal, but it got her moving forward again.

"What do you think, old girl?" Bonita asked the mare as she brushed the dust and dirt from her coat. "How about we go for a nice run today?"

Jasmine was older but she still had some bursts of speed in her, and as a Thoroughbred, she had a body built for running.

Instead of grabbing her English saddle, Bonita hoisted her new, custom Western saddle on her hip. It weighed a lot more and she had a bit of a challenge lugging the thing around—yet she had discovered that it was the more comfortable ride on the Montana terrain. She saddled the horse and then swung onto the Thoroughbred's back.

As she walked the horse toward one of the open fields, Bonita breathed in the fresh air and admired the untouched beauty of the land around her. As far as the eye could see was Delafuente land and it gave her a sense of ownership—a sense of pride—that she had never felt for this land before. For the longest time, this was her mother's dream—this was her mother's place. Had this land, quietly and without her consent, bored into her heart? Montana had certainly changed her on the outside at the very least.

She hadn't worn her breeches for months and her tall English riding boots were collecting dust in the back of her closet. Now her standard uniform was a pair of jeans, albeit designer, her second pair of ornately stitched cowgirl boots, a button-down blouse with the sleeves rolled up and her cream-colored straw cowgirl hat. She was as comfortable with these clothes now as she used to be in high heels and pencil skirts.

But, if she were truly honest with herself, Montana had done much more than change her appearance on the outside—it had changed her, for the better, on the inside. Montana was where she had grown into her skin as a woman. Montana, in some small way, had become her home.

She warmed up the mare at a walk and made her neck supple before she worked her at the trot. Jasmine had lost some condition, and Bonita knew, especially for an older horse, that she needed to increase her exercise program. Jasmine was her mom's pride and joy, a tangible connection to her mother. Bonita planned to honor her mother by caring for her beloved mare for the rest of Jasmine's life.

Bonita galloped the mare along the fence line that followed the long, winding driveway leading to the main road.

"Good girl, Jazz!" She patted the horse on the neck

with a laugh. It was exhilarating to gallop a horse in wide-open spaces with the Montana mountains in the background. She had spent her time riding in arenas— this was a whole different experience.

On her way back, she heard the sound of car tires on the gravel driveway. She spun Jasmine around and saw her father driving toward her. Smiling, she waved her arm in greeting, "Dad!"

George stopped on the other side of the fence and rolled down the window.

"*Mija!* This is how I wanted to see you!"

"Do you want to race?" Bonita asked her father with a smile. She knew, instinctively, that her father needed to see that she was okay. He had flown in specifically to check on her, even though she told him several times that it was unnecessary.

"Loser buys lunch," he said.

Bonita spun Jasmine around, leaned forward, gave the Thoroughbred her head and signaled for the mare to gallop. Jasmine bolted forward and raced George's car, neck and neck, all the way up the drive. The wind made her eyes tear, and the horse's speed made her heart race, and Bonita was laughing harder than she could remember laughing for many, many months. At the last moment, Jasmine pulled ahead and Bonita won the race.

"Woo-hoo!" Bonita raised both hands in the air triumphantly. "Lunch is on Dad!"

She swung out of the saddle, loosened the girth and then walked the mare to where her father was waiting for them.

"Look at you, *mija*! The *vaquero* blood is thick in your veins!" Her father hugged her tightly.

Before she could speak, he tightened his hold on her,

squeezing the air out of her lungs. "Don't disappear on me again, Bonita. I need to know you're safe. I can't lose you, too."

"I promise." She had been so deep in her own depression that she hadn't been able to think how her withdrawal from the world would impact her father.

George stepped away from her, a smile on his round face. "You look healthy. I was expecting to find a mess."

"Thanks, Dad." She rolled her eyes at him playfully.

She led the mare into the barn, unsaddled her, rinsed the sweat from her body and then turned her out into the pasture. When she met back up with her father, she asked, "What did you mean by my *vaquero* blood?"

"Your great-grandfather and your great-grandmother were both *vaqueros*. Many of your ancestors were *vaqueros*. Our people were the first cowboys—the best horsemen in the world."

"And horsewomen."

"Yes, *por supuesto!*" her father agreed.

After going into Bozeman for lunch, they returned to the ranch house. This was the first time since Evelyn's funeral that they had been in the house together.

"It's strange, isn't it?" Bonita asked her father in a whisper. Whenever she came into her mother's suite of rooms, she felt compelled to whisper, as if she were in a place of worship.

George's eyes were watery with loss. "It is as empty as I feel."

She hugged her father in response. Although her mother's scent had lingered for several days after her passing, that last lingering remnant of her mother was gone now.

"I'm going to start packing up her clothes. You know

how she felt about anything sitting around not being used for six months."

"Toss it," he said with a fond smile.

"She wanted us to donate the clothing."

He nodded his agreement.

Almost as a natural progression, they left the suite of rooms and walked together to the great room and stood in the spot where Evelyn had spent much of her time. They looked out the wall of windows that provided spectacular views of the ranch.

"What are you going to do with this place?" she asked her father.

George didn't respond right away—he seemed lost in thought.

"I don't know," he said finally. "I thought that I would immediately sell. But..."

"You feel her here," Bonita finished his sentence.

Her father turned his head away and swiped at his eyes quickly. He cleared his throat. "Yes. I feel my Evelyn here. And if my love is here," George gestured to the house and the land. "I can never sell."

After her father's visit, Bonita got down to the business of packing up her mother's closet. Evelyn had left specific instructions—she did not want her things collecting dust when "someone who was still breathing" could put them to perfectly good use. It was a huge chore, and one that came with frequent emotional breakdowns and tears, but she got it done. Bonita finished taping up the last box of clothes and checked her phone.

"Shoot!" she said out loud. "I've got to go!"

Gabe had invited her to Sugar Creek Ranch for his family's Sunday brunch and she had happily accepted.

The house was so lonely now; she couldn't wait to be surrounded by the cowboy's family. And, in particular, she was looking forward to seeing Liam's wife, Kate, again.

She checked her makeup and her hair in the hallway mirror, grabbed her purse and keys and headed out to her SUV. The plan was for her to meet Gabe at Little Sugar Creek and then they would drive over to his family's main ranch house together. It did occur to her that she was officially meeting the family but she was so hungry for *people* that she didn't feel all that nervous. Plus, she already knew Liam and Shane and Kate. If the rest of his family was anything like the first three, she was going to get along with them just fine.

"Hi!" She jumped out of her Range Rover and waved at Gabe. "I'm sorry I'm late!"

Gabe was sitting on the porch with Tater on his lap. He stood up, a smile on his handsome face, and greeted her at the top of the stairs.

She kissed Tater first and then tilted her head back for a kiss from the cowboy.

"Tater gets the first kiss?" Gabe's mouth quirked up into a playful smile.

"That goes without saying."

He put his arm around her and pulled her in for a sweet, long kiss.

"Hi, there," he said, his blue eyes staring into hers.

"Hi, there."

"Are you ready for a lot of food and a lot of loud talking?"

"Sounds like heaven."

Bonita loved her big family on her father's side— when they got together with all of the cousins and the aunts and the uncles, there was laughing and dancing, great food and of course, the occasional disagreement. But that was what was so wonderful about it. To be with another big family was exactly what Bonita felt like she needed right now.

They hopped into Gabe's truck with Tater sitting in her lap. He drove down his bumpy driveway to the main road, took a left and in a mile turned onto a well-kept paved driveway. The winding road leading up to the main ranch house at Sugar Creek took them through a scenic journey that reminded Bonita of a state park.

"This is incredible."

"Pop spent a lot of years building this ranch."

"And all of your siblings live here?"

"He carved off a piece of Sugar Creek for each one of his kids. Some of us settled here, others didn't."

Along the way, they passed herds of cattle and herds of horses, hay barns and pole barns housing large farm equipment. But Bonita was not prepared for what she saw as they drove up to the main ranch house.

She looked over at Gabe, a bit perplexed. It had never occurred to her that he came from a wealthy family. By the looks of Little Sugar Creek, she had the opinion that he was a man of modest means and he'd certainly never alluded to a wealthy family. But there was no doubt about it—the Brand family was rolling in it.

"Your father must do very well for himself." She stared at Gabe's profile.

He shifted into Park and cut off the engine. "He's picked up a few bucks along the way, that's for sure."

More than a few bucks. The house looked like a small resort with rustic dark brown wood, stone and walls of glass. It had to be at least eight thousand square feet under the main roof and that didn't include the multiple decks and large gazebo.

The house manager, Rosario, who obviously had a genuine affection for Gabe, greeted them at the door. When Bonita detected a bit of an accent in Rosario's English, she introduced herself in Spanish; the house manager's face lit up with delight and the two of them carried on a quick conversation.

"I heard my name." Gabe took his hat off and hung it on the rack near the door. "What did you ask Rosario?"

"I just asked if she thought you were a nice guy, is all."

"And?"

She leaned her head on his shoulder for a brief second. "She told me to run for the hills."

The inside of the house was an assault on the senses—everywhere you looked, there was texture and wood and decorations crafted by local artisans. The vertical beams supporting part of the second floor were all actual, massive tree trunks. The decor was heavily influenced by a Western motif, but there were lovely Native American accents throughout.

Gabe took her hand and they walked together to a banquet room with an enormous table. The family had already gathered, but it appeared that they had waited to serve the food until Bonita and Gabe arrived.

The moment his family saw them, everyone greeted them loudly and enthusiastically, urging them to sit down and join them. Before they took their seats at the long table, Gabe introduced her to his father, Jock, and his mother, Lilly.

"Good to know you," Jock said in a gruff, gravelly voice. He wasn't a tall man, but he cut an impressive figure with his barrel chest, leathery, wrinkled skin, his hawkish nose and white hair. His eyes were deep set and the same shocking aqua blue as his son's.

"Welcome." Lilly gave her a kind smile. "We are so happy to have you with us."

Lilly Hanging Cloud, Gabe's stepmother, was a full-blooded Chippewa-Cree Native American who had been raised on a Montana reservation. She had a lovely face with prominent cheekbones and she wore her silver-laced, black, bone-straight hair parted down the middle.

Gabe held out Bonita's chair for her and then he sat down. While platter after platter of food was served, he introduced her to his younger half brother Colton, a rancher to the core, and his oldest brother, Bruce. Savannah, Bruce's wife, was a pretty redhead. She held their sweet new baby daughter, Amanda, who appeared to be a ginger as well. Liam and Kate were at the table, so there were some familiar faces. Jessie, the only daughter as well as the youngest sibling, was tall, lanky and undeniably beautiful; she had her mother's features and coloring, silky long hair and her father's blue eyes.

"Shane's not coming?" Bonita asked Gabe, disappointed not to see the moody musician at the table. She had wanted to thank him again for his moving tribute to her mother at the funeral.

"He's not one for brunch," he told her, but she had the distinct feeling that he had left a lot unsaid.

The Brand family was a boisterous, loud, combative group that made Bonita feel like she was right at home. The food was different from what her father's side of the family would serve, but the talking and laughing at a deafening decibel was comforting to her.

Jock, who spoke in a booming voice, addressed her from his end of the table, "Bonita." He said her name slowly and in segments, and it came out like *Bow. Need. A.*

"That right there is one hundred percent Grade A Sugar Creek prime cut."

Bonita looked at a platter in front of her filled with thinly sliced pieces of beef.

"She's a vegetarian," Gabe told him.

"What was that?" Jock tilted his head toward his son as if he wanted to be able to hear him better.

"Jeez, Dad! Seriously, get your hearing checked!" Jessie didn't look up from her phone, which she had sitting on the table next to her plate. "She doesn't eat meat!"

Jock's deeply lined face puckered as he dropped his elbow on the table with a thud and pointed his finger at Bonita. "Now, young lady—that just ain't normal."

Bonita was about to respond when Gabe said, "There are plenty of people out there who don't eat meat, Dad. It's perfectly normal."

"Well." Jock grumbled. "They should if they knew what was good for them."

"Actually, Dad," Jessie chimed in. "Studies show that eating too much red meat is bad for you."

"Nonsense!" The man at the head of the table said in a loud voice. "I've eaten meat all my life for breakfast, lunch, and dinner, and I still work twelve hours a day." He turned his attention back to Bonita. "Now, just try a piece of this here prime grass-fed beef and see if doesn't change your life."

"I can't promise to try it." Bonita smiled at Jock, liking him even in his gruffness. "But, I will promise to admire it from afar."

Other than offending Jock by not eating a Sugar Creek steak, meeting Gabe's family felt easy and uncomplicated. She just fit in. She had a chance to catch up with Kate and they made a plan to meet for lunch in Bozeman the following week. In particular, Bonita liked Lilly.

"I love your moccasins." Bonita noticed a finely made pair of soft beaded shoes peeking out beneath the hem of Lilly's prairie skirt. "Whose are they?"

She was asking for the name of the designer, but Lilly looked at her a bit confused before she answered, "They're mine."

That made her laugh. "No. I mean, who made them?"

"I did."

"*You* made those?" Bonita was blown away by the craftsmanship of the moccasins. "That's incredible."

Savannah was walking by, stopped and said, "Lilly makes the most amazing handcrafted jewelry and clothing. She made my wedding dress—I'll have to show it to you sometime. It's living artwork."

Lilly was kind enough to take Bonita to her craft room and show her some of her creations. Bonita had an eye for well-designed, high-end fashion and Lilly's work was exquisite. The beading and the designs, all handcrafted, were truly special.

"Do you sell these?"

"Yes," Lilly said as she looked through a heavy, wooden trunk. "I donate the proceeds to my tribe—all of this funds scholarships for students to attend college."

"I know fashion," Bonita told her. "You could make a killing if you were in some of the high-end boutiques in DC."

"Please try these." Lilly held up a pair of heavily

beaded moccasins. "If these fit, I would like for you to have them."

Bonita was silent for a second or two, stunned by the offer of the beautiful moccasins. She took them, slipped off her boots and slipped on the moccasins.

"They fit!"

"Then they are meant for you to have and enjoy."

Bonita spontaneously hugged Lilly. "You have to let me pay you for them. It's too much."

Lilly refused to take any money. "This is my repayment of your gift."

"What gift?"

"We haven't had Gabe with us for a summer in so many years. He is here with us now because of you."

Gabe couldn't have known what it would be like to see Bonita with his family. He hadn't had a significant other at the family brunch for years; it had been difficult to watch his brothers with their wives and families, knowing that his love hadn't been put in his path.

But then along came beautiful, class act, intelligent Bonita. She was smart and funny and his family had accepted her without hesitation into their fold. It was particularly important to him that Lilly, whom he called Mom even though she was his stepmother, liked Bonita. To make a gift of her handcrafted moccasins, a skill that had been passed down to her through the generations of artisans at Rocky Boy Reservation, was all the validation he needed from Lilly.

After breakfast, he and Bonita returned to Little Sugar Creek, and she had a chance to spend some time with Val. Her bond with the massive Oldenburg had progressed nicely, but Gabe would still like to see some smoothing out of Val's bad behaviors before he returned to the Delafuente ranch full-time.

After training, Gabe was able to talk Bonita into his cabin and into his bed. He stripped her out of her clothes, starting at her neck and kissing his way downward, loving the scent of her of skin and the taste of her body.

She took charge, pushing him back on the bed and using those well-developed thighs to straddle him like her own personal stallion. While he watched, she rode him, taking her pleasure, moving her hips slowly. She was, in his mind, a goddess. A gorgeous, sexy, curvaceous goddess.

They loved each other until they were exhausted and sweaty and entirely spent. Laughing, Bonita rolled onto the bed beside him and curled her body toward his. Still breathing heavy from the effort he'd just exerted pleasuring his woman, Gabe turned to his side to face the woman of his dreams.

He reached out and touched her lovely face and then kissed her gently. "How do you say *I love you* in Spanish?"

"*Te amo.*"

With his hand still on her face, Gabe stared into Bonita's eyes so she would feel, in her heart, the sincerity of the words as he said, "*Te amo*, Bonita."

He was rewarded with a sweet, pleased smile. "*Te amo, tambien.* I love you, too."

## Chapter Fifteen

Bonita believed that she had accomplished everything that needed to be accomplished to fulfill her mother's wishes regarding her physical possessions. Evelyn's will had been executed and all inheritors addressed. Most of Evelyn's extensive jewelry collection went to Bonita and she decided to have her father secure the jewelry in a vault in their DC family home. Everything had been handled, with the exception of Jasmine and Val.

Now that her mother had passed, Bonita's job in Montana was over. Yes, they had decided to keep the ranch in the family, but the place could be managed with a ghost staff. She wasn't needed here anymore. So the question was—where was her next step and what plans needed to be made for the horses? Bonita wasn't superstitious, but a reminder email in her inbox seemed to arrive at the exact moment she was at a mental crossroads. And it did feel as if Evelyn was giving her a nudge from beyond.

The day the email arrived, Bonita visited her mother's grave to exchange the old flowers with fresh. Kneeling by the headstone, she touched the ornately carved marble, still in pristine condition, and wished that her mother could still be with her. Evelyn always gave her the best advice and she had a big decision to make.

"I have to decide, Mom. My acceptance to George-town expires next week."

She had two semesters post-acceptance to join the program without going through the application process again. When she'd first arrived in Montana, the idea of *not* immediately jumping at the chance to attend such a prestigious program would have been unthinkable. But that was before Montana had made its indelible impression on her heart—that was before she had fallen in love with a cowboy.

"What would you tell me to do?"

Bonita stood up with a sigh and stared at her mother's headstone a moment longer before turning and walking away. It seemed that no matter what she decided, she was going to lose something—or someone.

"This is the one." Gabe studied the engagement ring closely. It was an antique setting in platinum with an old-mine-cut diamond that had a rounded-square shape with fifty-eight hand cut facets. It was a class act of a ring for a class act of a woman.

"Bruce said this was coming, but I didn't believe him." Liam had met him at the jewelry store in down-town Bozeman. Bruce and Liam had bought rings for their wives from the same store, so Gabe figured that a third time would bring some charm to his purchase.

He gave the clerk his credit card, confident in his decision about the ring and the woman he intended to make his bride.

"I didn't really see it coming," he told his brother. "But they say when you know, you know."

"Kate loves her. So does Mom."

"That's important."

"It sure is," Liam agreed.

The clerk brought the receipt for him to sign, along with a small bag that held the key to his future.

"Congratulations." The clerk smiled at him as she took the signed receipt.

Gabe put his hat back on and tipped it to her. "I appreciate your help."

Outside the store, Liam asked, "When are you going to ask her?"

"Tonight."

"Tonight?" His brother seemed surprised. "That's fast, brother."

"Maybe. But I don't see what the point of waiting is. She'll either say yes or she'll say no."

"What are you leaning toward?"

Gabe laughed. "Well, I'm leaning toward yes obviously."

At the point where they were about to part ways, Liam faced him and had a serious look on his face. "The one thing that worries me, Gabe, is that you told me yourself she didn't plan on staying in Montana."

"That was a while back."

That's what Gabe said out loud, but his brother managed to land on his main concern about his relationship with Bonita. They were living in the moment, not really addressing the future, and that had been fine with him—until it wasn't fine for him any longer. He believed that all evidence pointed to Bonita having the potential to be very happy in Montana, with him, but it was an open question as to whether or not she would choose that path.

Liam was one of his more cerebral, diplomatic brothers, so he didn't push the issue. Instead he gave him a hug and wished him good luck.

"Hey." Gabe tried to cover up his worry with humor. "She can't turn me down if I don't ask."

Gabe had on a new suit when he picked her up for dinner. Up until that point, she had only seen him in his one every-occasion-wedding-or-funeral suit.

"You look really handsome, Gabe."

He was still wearing cowboy boots and a cowboy hat with the suit, but they were new and fit the ensemble.

"You look especially lovely tonight." He was always quick to compliment her.

She hadn't really had an occasion to put on more glamorous makeup and wear her stilettos for a while. Gabe had said he was taking her to a restaurant with a dress code, which gave her the perfect excuse to wear one of her DC dresses and glam herself up a bit.

She gave him a little twirl so he could get the full view. As she always did, she felt happy to see him. And she hoped that the night would end on a positive note for both of them.

When they got in his truck, country music came on the radio. Gabe reached over to shut it off.

"That's okay. You can play it low."

He gave her an odd look that made her laugh.

"Don't get all excited. I still hate it," she told him. "Just not as much as I used to."

Gabe had reservations for them at the Emerson Grill.

The scent of the food and the warm ambience of the restaurant were a hit with Bonita right away.

"Italian?" she asked as they were led to a small booth tucked away in a corner.

Gabe waited for her to take her seat before he joined her. "You said it was your favorite."

"I love it. Second only to authentic Mexican cuisine."

Gabe had done his homework because he knew the sweetest red wine on the menu and he ordered them a bottle.

"I'm impressed," she told him after they ordered appetizers and their entrée.

"You matter to me." He held out his wineglass so they could toast. "To many more evenings like this one."

Bonita touched her glass to his, but her free hand went to her stomach and her fingers curled into a fist. She had something that she needed to tell Gabe—a decision she had made about her future—but she had wanted to wait for another time. She had known that he had gone to an awful lot of trouble to spoil her with a fancy night out on the town.

"I was working with Val today," Gabe said.

She put her glass down on the table, glad for a change of subject to a neutral topic.

"I think he's ready," he went on.

"Ready?"

"To go back to the ranch with you. Jasmine needs the company and now you've got a little room to breathe in your schedule. I figured this was the right time."

Her stomach clenched. A conversation about bringing Val back to the ranch was inevitably going to lead into another topic that she wanted to avoid.

"I don't know. Maybe." She felt like a real jerk giving him that wimpy answer, especially when she knew it was a lie. Gabe had always been straight with her—he'd always told her the unvarnished truth. He deserved the same from her.

His face changed. Up until that moment, he had been in a great mood—laughing, joking and admiring her with his beautiful aqua blue eyes. But, he was sharp—much sharper than she had realized when they first met. Her answer had set off an alarm bell in the man's head and she could see it on his face.

"Maybe?" he repeated, sitting back in the booth. "You used to be anxious to get him back on the ranch with you."

There was a definite question hanging in the air between them. Bonita breathed in deeply and blew the breath out slowly. She folded her hands in her lap; she was not going to get through the dinner as planned without broaching a potentially damaging subject. She loved Gabe—but the truth was, she didn't really know how to make their relationship work long-term. Not really.

"Actually," she said, her heart beating anxiously, "Val isn't going to be coming back to the ranch. He's going back to Virginia."

Gabe didn't say a word; he was waiting for her to finish, seeming to gauge each one of her words very carefully.

"Look—he's doing great with you. But he's not a ranch horse. He needs to be at a facility with people who can keep him on a strict training program. That's just not going to happen here. And let's face it, Val and I are doing better, but we've never clicked. I think this will be what's best for everyone. Especially Val."

"I'll look at my schedule and see when I can haul him back."

"Thank you."

Gabe poured himself some more wine and topped off her glass as well. He seemed a bit more relaxed, but he seemed warier.

"When I get back, I'll help you find a good solid ranch horse so Jasmine has some company out there."

Bonita's hand tightened on the stem of the glass. "Well… Jasmine is going to Virginia, too."

The waitress brought out the antipasto, briefly interrupting their conversation. Neither of them reached for the food.

"You aren't keeping Jasmine with you?"

Quietly, Bonita said, "I am keeping her with me."

She knew she was going to hurt him. She knew that she was going to hurt herself. But she wasn't prepared for the look she saw in his eyes—he looked like someone punched him in the gut. Maybe in his mind he knew there was a good chance she would be leaving Bozeman; it was clear to her that his heart hadn't believed it was possible.

Bonita reached across the table to put her hand on his. He didn't pull away but he didn't take her hand in kind. After a second, she pulled back.

"I didn't want to bring this up tonight. I really didn't. But, you brought up Val coming back to the ranch, and I don't want to lie to you."

"When did you decide all of this?" he asked, his jaw clenched.

"Today. This afternoon." He didn't seem to have anything to say, so she added, "My admission to medical school was about to expire."

She sensed that there were no words she could say to make the news any more palatable for him. He sat across from her, tapping his finger on the table. He didn't look at her for what seemed like an hour, even though it was only minutes. Finally, he cleared his throat and caught her gaze.

"*Te amo*, Bonita." Gabe held up his wineglass in a second toast. "You're going to make one hell of a fine doctor."

Gabe hung his hat on the hook just inside of his door and jerked the knot in his tie loose. He pulled the tie off his neck, tossed it on the table next to the door and then picked up Tater, who was waiting to be loved. He carried the dog over to the couch and sat down heavily. Tater licked his cheek, which made him smile, just a little bit.

"I was expecting a different kind of kiss tonight, Tater."

He envied the dog in that moment. Her life was uncomplicated. She ate, she slept, and she got a lot of love. End of story. He, on the other hand, was in love with a woman who was leaving the state—perhaps for good.

"Let me get out of this monkey suit, Tater." Gabe sighed.

He went into the sleeping quarters, kicked off his dress shoes, shrugged out of his suit jacket and stripped off his slacks. He pulled on a pair of old jeans but didn't bother to put on a shirt or boots. He hung up his suit jacket and reached into the pocket to pull out the small ring box. He opened the lid, looked at the antique engagement ring before he tossed the box into one of the closet drawers. He'd had a much different ending planned for this night.

Gabe grabbed a beer out of the refrigerator and went out onto the porch. Meeting Bonita—loving Bonita—let him know that he was tired, dog-tired, of being alone. He was ready for more. But how could he think about having *more* with anyone other than Bonita—a woman who appeared to be just out of his reach?

Five beers later on a mostly empty stomach, Gabe was feeling a mixture of sorrow and anger. He wasn't mad at Bonita—she was doing exactly what she told him all along she was going to do, going back to her life in DC. No. He was pissed off at himself. He had lied to himself about the relationship and that just wasn't like him.

"Where the leather is scarred, there's a great story to tell." He lifted his sixth bottle of beer to the night.

Gabe stood up, wobbled a bit and then chugged the last beer in his six-pack. He was about to head in when he saw headlights turn into his drive. The closer the headlights got, the clearer he could see the vehicle. It was Bonita's Range Rover.

He felt foggy-headed as his love walked toward him.

"I didn't like the way we left things," she said, her loose, long hair blowing gently around her shoulders. She looked so pretty standing there that it broke his heart.

"I really love you, Gabe." Bonita was on the bottom step now.

She must have seen him sway to the side because she was suddenly standing next to him, her arm around his waist. "Are you drunk?"

His knees felt rubbery now that he was trying to stand upright for more than a minute. "A bit."

"How'd you get drunk so fast? You just dropped me off!"

Gabe burped. "Talent."

Bonita helped him inside, took the empty bottle out of his hand, and he fell backward onto the mattress. She unbuttoned and unzipped his pants and helped him out of them.

"We aren't going to get any talking done tonight," she said.

Gabe heard her voice only after he woke himself up with a snore. He reached out for her. "Come here and love on me, woman."

Gabe had passed out before she got into bed with him and he was still asleep when she awakened. She found some fixings for breakfast, made a pot of strong coffee and had everything ready for him by the time he came wandering into the kitchen. His hair was rumpled and he was yawning while he scratched his chest.

"Good morning." She handed him a cup of coffee.

He looked at her through squinty, bloodshot eyes as if he was unclear about what she was doing in his cabin.

"Have a seat," she told him. "I'll bring you your breakfast."

He ate in silence and Bonita let him work through his kinks. He was obviously hungover. Gabe cleaned his plate, pushed it out of his way and drank the rest of his coffee.

He put down his empty cup and then he was staring at her. The intensity of his gaze—the intensity of the examination of her face—made her shift in her chair.

"I'm pissed off at you," he said bluntly.

"I know."

He leaned forward on his elbows. "I was thinking that it was time for us to start talking about getting married."

She didn't repeat the word *married* aloud, but it bounced around in her brain like a loose BB.

"Damn it, Bonita. Don't look at me like I just asked you to commit a crime."

"I'm not! I'm just surprised that you think we're even ready for that."

"It's not complicated. I love you, you love me."

But it was much more complicated than that. "Look, Gabe. I do love you. But I didn't move to Montana by choice. I came here because my mom was sick and she needed me."

He listened while she continued.

"I put my plans for medical school on hold. I never intended to give my dreams up entirely. And I know you say it doesn't matter to you—the chance that I could get sick—but it matters to me." She pointed at her chest. "What happened to my mom could happen to me, and while I still can, I'm going to live *now*. I'm not going to wait. I have to do this for myself and I have to do it for my mom."

She wiped tears out of her eyes—the loss of her mom still fresh. "I never planned on staying here."

She looked up and Gabe had that punched-in-the-gut expression on his face.

"I don't want to hold you back from your dreams, Bonita," he said. "But we started something here and you can't deny that. Maybe you never planned on staying here. I get that. But, here's the million-dollar question that I need answered—do you ever plan on coming back?"

It took her several long seconds to respond in a quiet voice, "I don't know."

"You said you didn't want to lie to me." Gabe pinned her with those blue eyes of his.

Her eyebrows drew together and she frowned at him. "I *don't know*, Gabe! I just lost my mom and I feel like I have to relearn how to do everything without her. I need time to figure things out. That's what I know. I also know that I love you, I don't want this to be good-bye, but I have been accepted to one of the best medical programs in the county. I want to become a doctor and nothing is going to stand in the way of that."

"I'm not looking to end things. Far the hell from it," Gabe said, his face tense. "But this is what I know, Bonita. I'm a Montana man. This is my home. If you don't think, after you finish school, that you could come back here and be happy, then I've got no choice but to let you go."

## Chapter Sixteen

One of the many things Bonita learned about Gabe Brand was that he was the consummate gentleman. She had the feeling that Lilly was responsible for instilling this invaluable trait in her son. Even when he was hurt or angry or disappointed, Gabe did the right thing by the women in his life. She had firsthand experience with this.

After trying to hash things out, they had both come to the decision that they should give their relationship some room to breathe. They weren't cutting ties completely, but they were accepting the reality that their lives were heading, for the time being at least, in very different directions.

In light of that decision, Bonita had wanted to hire a different long distance transporter to move Val and Jasmine back to Virginia. Gabe wouldn't hear of it. It didn't matter to him that their relationship had taken an unexpected turn; he wanted to personally see to it that her horses were safely delivered to their new home. So they had taken another four-day journey together in his rig; the place where they had first formed a friendship. The place where they had first formed a bond.

It wasn't the same trip as before. How could it be? There was a poignant heaviness in the air between them, but it wasn't all doom and gloom. They couldn't help but make each other laugh, and even though things were uncertain between them, their physical chemistry pulled them back into each other's arms before the trip was over. For Bonita, the lovemaking had been the most passionate and intimate and intense of her life. They made love to each other as if it were for the last time, because they both knew that it just might be.

"How are classes?" Her friend Jill joined her for coffee weeks later. "Crazy?"

"It feels like someone backed up a dump truck and unloaded a ton of work on top of me," Bonita said with a laugh. "But I love it."

"Did you hear anything about the research position?"

"I got it!"

"Bonita!" Jill's face lit up. "Congratulations! That's a really big deal."

It was a really big deal. Bonita had managed to secure a position as a research assistant for one of the program professors and it was a prestigious appointment.

Her first semester of medical school was off to a busy but successful start. Her move back to DC had gone smoothly. Jasmine and Val were settled into the facility in Alexandria; she had decided to find Val a permanent rider with an option to buy to keep him on the show circuit and Jasmine was signed up for regular exercise as well. She had purchased a penthouse apartment near Howard Theatre, restaurants and shopping. In theory, she had it all. But in reality, she didn't because she didn't have Gabe.

She drank coffee and caught up with the new events in Jill's life for another hour before Bonita knew she had to get back to her studies. There were plenty of nightlife options all around her, yet the chances of having much of a social life while she was in school were less than zero.

Bonita opened the door to her apartment and was greeted by her new feline friend, a long-haired rescue named Patch. Patch was all white, except for a black marking around his left eye that looked exactly like a pirate's patch. He was ten years old and came with the name, but it seemed to fit.

Bonita picked up the cat and hugged him. He sat in her arms, purring and rubbing his face against hers.

"How are you, my handsome boy?" She kissed him on the head.

She grabbed another cup of coffee, which she now consumed morning, afternoon and night, and went to her office. There were books stacked up to eye level on her desk and there were piles of research articles everywhere.

Patch followed her into the office, jumped up on the desk and took his favorite spot beneath the lamp, right next to the wedding photo of her parents.

"All right." Bonita sighed. "Let's get some work done."

She tried to read one of the many chapters assigned for the week, but she discovered that the street noise was distracting her and she ended up reading the same paragraph several times without actually comprehending the content.

"Ah!" She hit the book with her hands in frustration. "It's so *noisy* here, Patch!"

She had been so excited to get back to the city, to the energy of the place. But what she hadn't anticipated was how much she was going to miss the quiet of Montana. Before Bozeman, she hadn't noticed the noise that came from living with people in closer quarters. Now, every sound, from the voices on the street below to the honking of the cars to the doors shutting in the hallway drove her nuts.

"Fine." She opened the desk drawer and grabbed the pair of expensive noise-canceling headphones her father had sent her the week before. It was annoying to have to wear headphones just to hear herself thinking!

Bonita read chapters and took notes until she couldn't stand to do it for a minute longer. With Patch in tow, she retired for the night. She was too tired to take a shower, but she brushed her teeth and took care of her skin. Once she was in bed, she set the alarm on her phone and then started her evening ritual. First, she listened to an old message that she had saved on her phone from her mother. Missing her mother was a constant ache and being able to hear her voice—being able to still hear her say, *"Te amo, mija"*—was a gift.

"Good night, Mom." She pressed her fingers to her lips and then transferred the kiss to a small oval framed picture of her mother.

"Are you comfortable?" Bonita petted her feline companion, who had curled up beside her on top of the blanket. She switched off the light, and then put her earbuds in and turned on the music she listened to every night before she went to bed: country.

It seemed ridiculous, but listening to the music she

knew Gabe loved made her feel close to him; especially now when they couldn't be farther apart, literarily and figuratively. After a heated phone conversation, he had told her that he needed to take some time away from the relationship. It had been a month since she had spoken to him—he wasn't answering her texts, returning her calls or responding to her emails. He had, for all intents and purposes, ended things between them.

When she was in class or working or studying, it was easy to push aside the pain of losing her mother and Gabe. That was far from the case when it was time to sleep. No matter how exhausted she was, sleep didn't come easy. Gabe was the last person she thought of before she fell asleep, and he was often the first person on her mind when she awakened. She told Jill as much the next day when they had a few minutes to chat on the phone.

"I miss him," she told her friend. "He's just a genuinely kind man. He makes me feel cherished and loved and safe when I'm with him. And I know—truly know— that if I do get sick that he'd be there for me. He'd take care of me. I never thought I'd actually be able to say that about anyone."

"That's hard to find."

Some women waited their whole lives for Mr. Right to come along, only to be disappointed. From her perspective, Mr. Right came unexpectedly at the wrong time in her life. But maybe it hadn't been the wrong time. Maybe he had come into her life at the exact time when she had needed him the most.

"I don't know what to do." As she said the words, she knew that wasn't true.

"What would your mom tell you to do?"

That was easy to answer. She would tell her what she had told her right up to the end of her life. "Don't be afraid to live your life."

"Good advice."

"Excellent advice," Bonita agreed. And then, just like a light turning on with a simple flick of a switch, she knew exactly what she needed to do to get back on track with the man she loved. "Hey, Jill. Would you be willing to watch Patch over the weekend? I think I need to go home."

After she hung up the phone with her friend, she called her dad. It might feel like Gabe was a world away right now, but he really wasn't. In fact, he was only a plane ride away.

"Dad—I need to borrow the jet."

Life after Bonita had left Montana felt hollow to Gabe. He still took pleasure in training horses and he had a couple of long-distance transports on the calendar, but his day-to-day existence seemed mundane. Days seemed to stretch out longer than normal and he found himself spending more time alone and going to bed before the sunset.

He'd never been truly depressed in his life, just normal ups and downs. But this thing was holding on for dear life; he didn't like it. More than that, he didn't like the twist in his gut every time he thought of Bonita— every time he imagined her face, the scent of her skin or the taste of her lips. He missed her in a way that didn't seem possible and the more he missed her, the more he wanted to push her away.

The last time they'd spoken, Bonita still couldn't say whether she would ever return to Montana. He couldn't change that part of him—he just couldn't. He was a fifth generation Montanan; this land was a part of his DNA. And if the love they shared wasn't strong enough to pull her back to him, then it wasn't a love strong enough to keep. So he walked away from her. It was the only thing he could do. He had to get down to the business of healing his heart.

"All right." Gabe lowered his rifle and looked at the target. "Now that felt good."

One way he was working through some of his angst was to run through boxes of ammo. He liked to shoot and he had plenty of guns to choose from. Some days, when he didn't have a client, he'd spend the afternoon shooting at a paper target until there was nothing left of it.

"That looks like a good way to relieve stress."

Gabe had just put his rifle down and had taken his ear protection off. He hadn't heard anyone come up the drive and he sure as heck wasn't expecting to hear anyone talking to him. Caught off guard, he stared at Bonita.

She was standing a few feet away from him, just as pretty as the day he first met her. But this time, she wasn't dressed in English riding gear. She was in jeans, cowgirl boots and the cowgirl hat he'd handpicked for her. His body immediately reacted to the sight of her— he couldn't stop himself from admiring the sexy curves of her hips and legs in those jeans. His first instinct was to grab her and hold her in his arms the way he had held her so many times in his daydreams.

She gave a little self-conscious wave. "Hi."

He picked up a new box of ammo. "You were just in the neighborhood?"

Bonita gave him a hesitant smile. "Well, I had to travel like two thousand miles to get into the neighborhood. But yeah. I was just in the neighborhood and I thought, hey, why don't I stop by and see my old friend, Gabe?"

His lost love was standing so close to him now that he could catch the subtle lavender scent of her hair. Gabe had to resist the urge to pull her into his arms—to kiss her.

"Can I try that?" she asked.

"Ever shot one?"

She laughed. "No. But it looks like fun."

He'd imagined her coming back into his life a hundred times, but he hadn't imagined it like this. Gabe selected a less powerful rifle for Bonita to shoot for the first time. He showed her how to hold it, how to aim and how to pull the trigger in one smooth motion.

"It's going to kick back against your shoulder. Don't brace against it but expect it," he told her as he put a spare set of headphones on her head and adjusted them. While he showed her how to hold the rifle, he had to put his arms around her, he had to touch her, and it hadn't taken much for his body to start betraying him.

"When you're ready," he instructed from a few paces away. "Go ahead and pull that trigger, nice and smooth."

Bonita shot the rifle, and as he'd warned her, the rifle jumped in her hand and kicked back against her shoulder. But when she looked over at him, her face was beaming with pleasure and she was smiling like someone who had just won a prize.

"Did you see that? I almost hit the target!"

He stepped forward and adjusted her grip and repositioned the rifle. "Keep her steady when you pull the trigger."

The second time Bonita shot the rifle, she hit the target. He'd never seen anyone so excited to hit a target before.

"I did it! Did you see that?"

"I saw it."

"I need to do that again. Is there still ammo in this thing? Do I need to reload?"

Gabe hadn't felt like laughing lately, but seeing Bonita take pure joy in one of his favorite activities made him smile. He taught her how to load the weapon and she kept on shooting until she could hit the target five times in a row.

"I think I'm really good at this." Bonita took off the headphones after she handed the rifle back to him.

"Seems like it."

Her hands on her hips, his love seemed buoyed. "I honestly never understood the point of all of this. But now I *get* it. I feel like I got all kinds of frustrations out."

Gabe packed up his guns and equipment and they walked toward the cabin.

"You want something to drink? I have wine."

"You're drinking wine now?"

"I don't drink it."

After drinking wine and chasing it with beer the night he had intended to propose, Gabe discovered that he was definitely not wired for wine.

"I keep a bottle around just in case." He didn't add that he had bought it for her—she was smart enough to figure that part out.

"Well, like my mom always said, it's five o'clock somewhere."

\* \* \*

Tater was happy to see her, and as she always had, Bonita doted on the little dog. Gabe popped the cork on a bottle of sweet red wine, the kind he knew she liked, and poured her a glass. He grabbed a beer out of the refrigerator and twisted off the top. They stood across the butcher-block island from each other; Gabe touched the bottom of his bottle to her glass.

"What are we toasting to?"

"Not a thing." He lifted the bottle to his mouth to take a swig.

She stopped him and held her glass up in the air. "To us."

He didn't join the toast. Up until she showed up on his property unannounced, he was under the impression that there wasn't any *us* any longer. He gave her a little nod and then took a drink.

It hadn't seemed awkward before, but it was feeling pretty awkward now. Bonita sent him a nervous smile. He wasn't used to seeing her acting nervous. That wasn't her style.

"You're probably wondering why I'm here."

"A bit."

Bonita took another sip of her wine and Gabe couldn't stop himself from imaging kissing the sweetness of it off her lips.

"I'm here because I love you, Gabe. I love you. I miss you." She gestured around her. "And no matter where I am in the world, my home is here…with you."

Her words—words he had thought to never hear from her—hit him in the heart. They gave him license to act on impulse and forgo formality. He put his bottle down on the island, walked the short distance to Bonita, took her wineglass from her hand, put it on the island and then picked her up in his arms and carried her, like he was carrying his bride over a threshold, toward his bedroom.

"What are you doing?" Bonita asked on a laugh.

"I'm taking you to bed."

"Don't you think we should finish talking?"

"No. Every time you talk, you screw things up between us."

"Every time *I* talk? Now wait just a minute!"

"Shhh."

"Did you just *shush* me?" She started to push on his chest. "You'd better put me down!"

He did put her down—right where he wanted her—on his bed.

She stared up at him and he stared right back as he said. "You came here to make up with me, so let's make up."

They could talk later; there would be plenty of time for that. But right now, his body ached for her. He was tired of lonely nights and frustrating days. He wanted to make love to his woman and show her how much he had missed her.

Gabe wrapped her up in his arms in a gentle tackle until they were both lying down on the bed. He held her in his arms and she felt so damn good and he kissed away any words that were about to come out of her sweet mouth.

He pulled her into his body tighter, wanting to hold her so close. He kissed her neck, breathing in that lavender scent. "God, I've missed you."

When he lifted his head to look at her face, Bonita

looked him directly in the eye and said sincerely, "I have missed you every second of every day."

They stripped off their clothes; they didn't need anything between them. Gabe skipped the foreplay when he felt how ready she was for him; he fit himself between her thighs, slipped inside of her, deep and hard, until he heard her gasp in pleasure. He held her hands in his, their fingers joined together, as he thrust into her with long, deliberate strokes while she made small sexy noises in the back of her throat.

When she came for him, he lost himself inside her body, like a man who had finally found his way home. He was sweating and breathing heavy and she was laughing as she hugged him to her.

They took a quick shower together, cooling off their bodies. He kissed the water off her neck and her breasts, ending with a deep kiss on the lips before he left her to enjoy the shower on her own.

She was drying off with a towel when he returned with a glass of the wine she liked.

"I'm glad you're here," he said, enjoying the simple pleasure of watching her dry off with a towel. It was those small things of everyday life that he had really missed the most.

"I am, too." She wrapped her hair up into the towel like a turban and walked past him, naked, to get dressed.

He caught her by the waist to stop her from walking by. "Pay the toll."

She smiled at him and kissed him.

He turned to watch her dress. Now that the urgent need to bury himself deep within her had passed, his mind was starting to run through conversation scenarios, not all of them with happy endings.

They sat down together on the front step of the porch so they could watch the sunset. Bonita had taken her hair out of the towel, and now there were long, damp tendrils framing her face. How he adored his lovely Bonita. How he loved having her back at Little Sugar Creek with him. She was the missing piece to his puzzle.

"Did you mean it?" he asked her. "That Montana is your home?"

She stared out at the landscape before them, so quiet and pristine.

"Yes. I did mean it," Bonita said quietly. "Where Mom is, that's always been home to me. This is where she is now."

Then Bonita said, "And, this is where you are. I always knew how much I love you, Gabe. That was never a question in my mind. But I didn't know how much I loved this life I have with you here until I left it." She turned to him and he could read the sincerity in her soft, brown-black eyes. "I used to think that Washington, DC, and medical research were my future. But I don't think so anymore." She reached for his hand as she continued, "I've had a chance to be a part of medical research this semester, and as much as I've liked the experience, I just don't see myself doing that for the rest of my life. I want to interact with my patients in a more personal way. I want to see, firsthand and right away, how I impact their lives. That's what I want. And…" she met his eyes "…I can do that anywhere. I can do that right here in Bozeman."

"We're always hurting for good doctors," he told her. "You could do an awful lot of good for an awful lot of people."

Her brow wrinkled. "I never knew just how noisy the city is."

That made him laugh. He always missed the quiet of the ranch whenever he was in the city.

"If I opened a practice in Bozeman after I graduate…" she leaned toward him with a shy smile "…I could be your wife."

Gabe didn't trust that he had heard her correctly; the day had started out to be just another ordinary day. And, suddenly, it had become extraordinary.

"You want to get married?"

She leaned toward him and kissed him lightly on the lips. "I do."

"When?"

Bonita threaded her arm through his with a happy laugh. "When we're both ready, I suppose."

He stared at her for several seconds and then stood up abruptly.

"What's wrong?" His love had a worried expression on her face.

"Not a thing." He kissed her to reassure her. "I'll be right back."

At the door, he paused. "Don't you go anywhere."

He went to his dresser, opened the top drawer, and pushed a heap of socks and undershirts out of the way and found the box he had tried to forget at the very back of the drawer. He opened it and realized that he had purchased the perfect ring for the perfect woman—he had just planned to give it to her at an imperfect moment.

The sun was setting and his big Montana sky was bursting with brilliant reds and oranges—the perfect backdrop for one of the most important moments of his life.

He sat down beside her and took her hand into his hand.

"I know I don't pray as often as you'd like." He paused and ran his thumb over the empty spot on her ring finger that he hoped to fill.

In a raspy voice, he continued, "But, I've been praying every day for you to come home to me, Bonita."

She squeezed his hand, moving her body closer to his.

"It feels a little bit unreal that you're sitting here with me now, saying all the things that I've wanted to hear. But I don't want to let this moment pass me by. I love you, Bonita. I love you more today than I did yesterday, and that's just the truth of things. I know you've got school to finish back in Washington, but distance doesn't have to be a deal breaker for us. You can come to me and I can come to you, until we can be together full-time. When it comes to you, I've got plenty of patience."

"I want this to work, too, Gabe," she interjected, holding on tight to his hand.

With his free hand, he fished the ring out of his front pocket.

"I want to marry you, Bonita. Today, tomorrow, next year." Gabe said. "Will you marry me, *mi amor*?"

Bonita seemed surprised that he was able to call her "my love" in Spanish, just as she seemed surprised that he had just pulled an engagement ring out of his pocket. She stared at the sparkling diamond, for a couple of very long seconds before she looked up at him with unshed tears in her eyes.

There was a catch in her voice when she asked, "In sickness and in health?"

"Till death do us part."

"Yes, Gabe." She smiled at him with a small nod. "I want to marry you."

Gabe slipped the ring onto her finger and then they stood together and embraced. He kissed her cheeks and buried his face in her neck to breathe in the scent of the woman he loved. Bonita rested her head on the spot just over his heart and hugged him in a way that let him know that she wasn't ever going to let him go again.

"My beautiful, sweet Bonita. You have always had this cowboy's heart."

\* \* \* \* \*

*Be sure to look for*
Shane Brand's Christmas Mission,
*the next book in Joanna Sims's*
The Brands of Montana *miniseries,*
*available November 2018!*

*And catch up with the rest of the Brands in these*
*other great romances:*

Meet Me at the Chapel
Thankful for You
A Wedding to Remember
A Bride for Liam Brand

*Available now wherever Harlequin Special Edition*
*books and ebooks are sold.*

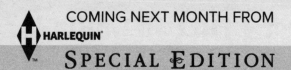

## COMING NEXT MONTH FROM

# HARLEQUIN®

# SPECIAL EDITION

### Available August 21, 2018

#### #2641 THE LITTLE MAVERICK MATCHMAKER
*Montana Mavericks: The Lonelyhearts Ranch* • by Stella Bagwell
Young Dillon Strickland has set his seven-year-old sights on making pretty
school librarian Josselyn Weaver a part of his family—by setting her up
with his father, Dr. Drew Strickland. The widower and the librarian have a lot
to overcome, but can a determined little boy set them on the path to
true love?

#### #2642 SIX WEEKS TO CATCH A COWBOY
*Match Made in Haven* • by Brenda Harlen
Kenzie Atkins refuses to fall for Spencer Channing—again. But she has no
defenses against his little girl, and her heart encourages her to lasso the
sexy cowboy—and round up a family!

#### #2643 FALLING FOR THE WRONG BROTHER
*Maggie & Griffin* • by Michelle Major
Runaway bride Mayor Maggie Spencer doesn't anticipate the fallout from
fleeing her wedding. Or her ex-fiancé's brother riding to her rescue!
Griffin Stone used to run from challenges, but now he'll have to fight—for
Maggie and their forbidden love.

#### #2644 SPECIAL FORCES FATHER
*American Heroes* • by Victoria Pade
Marine Liam Madison's world is rocked when he discovers that he's the
father of four-year-old twins. But it's their nanny, Dani Cooper, who might
just turn out to be the biggest surprise waiting for him in Denver.

#### #2645 HOW TO BE A BLISSFUL BRIDE
*Hillcrest House* • by Stacy Connelly
Nothing frightens photojournalist Chance McClaren more than the thought
of settling down. Can Alexa Mayhew convince this dad-to-be to set his
sights on family and forever?

#### #2646 THE SHERIFF OF WICKHAM FALLS
*Wickham Falls Weddings* • by Rochelle Alers
Deputy Sheriff Seth Collier wasn't looking for love, but when the beautiful
new doctor in town, Natalia Hawkins, moves in next door, he's more than
tempted to change his mind. But Natalia is coming off a bad breakup and
she's not sure she'll ever trust another man again.

---

**YOU CAN FIND MORE INFORMATION ON UPCOMING HARLEQUIN® TITLES,
FREE EXCERPTS AND MORE AT WWW.HARLEQUIN.COM.**

HSECNM0818

"What's going on here, Griffin?"

"I'm on an amazing date with an amazing woman and—"

"This isn't a date," she interrupted, tugging her hand from his.

He shifted, looking down into her gray eyes. Strands of lights lined the pier, so he could see that her gaze was guarded...serious. Not at all the easygoing, playful woman who'd sat across from him at dinner.

"You're sure?"

"I'm not sure of anything at the moment. You might remember my life turned completely upside down last week. But even if that wasn't a factor, I can't imagine you wanting to date me."

"I'm not the same guy I used to be."

She laughed softly. "I get that you were an angry kid and the whole 'rebel without a cause' bit."

"I hated myself," he admitted softly. "And I was jealous of you. You were perfect. Everyone in town loved you. It was clear even back then that you were the golden girl of Stonecreek, which meant you represented everything I could never hope to be."

"But now I'm okay because my crown has been knocked off?"

"That's not it," he said, needing her to understand. He paced to the edge of the pier then back to her. "I can't explain it but there's a connection between us, Maggie. I know you feel it."

She glanced out to the ocean in front of them. "I do."

"I think maybe I realized it back then. Except you were younger and friends with Trevor and so far out of my league." He chuckled. "That part hasn't changed. But I'm not the same person, and I want a chance with you."

"It's complicated," she said softly. "A week ago I was supposed to marry your brother. If people in town caught wind that I'd now turned my sights to you, imagine what that would do to my reputation."

The words were a punch to the gut. He might not care what anyone in Stonecreek thought about him, but it was stupid to think Maggie would feel the same way. She was the mayor after all and up for reelection in the fall. He stared at her profile for several long moments. Her hair had fallen forward so that all he could see was the tip of her nose. She didn't turn to him or offer any more of an explanation.

"I understand," he told her finally.

"I had a good time tonight," she whispered, "but us being together in Stonecreek is different."

"I get it." He made a show of checking his watch. "It's almost eleven. We should head back."

Her shoulders rose and fell with another deep breath. She turned to him and cupped his jaw in her cool fingers. "Thank you, Griffin. For tonight. I really like the man you've become." Before he could respond, she reached up and kissed his cheek.

*Don't miss*
Falling for the Wrong Brother *by Michelle Major,*
*available September 2018 wherever*
Harlequin® *Special Edition books and ebooks are sold.*

www.Harlequin.com

# *LOVE*
# Harlequin
# romance?

Join our Harlequin community to share your
thoughts and connect with other
romance readers!

Be the first to find out about promotions,
news, and exclusive content!

Sign up for the Harlequin e-newsletter and
download a free book from any series at

## www.TryHarlequin.com

---

**CONNECT WITH US AT:**

Harlequin.com/Community

 Facebook.com/HarlequinBooks

 Twitter.com/HarlequinBooks

 Instagram.com/HarlequinBooks

 Pinterest.com/HarlequinBooks

ReaderService.com

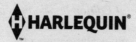

**ROMANCE WHEN
YOU NEED IT**

HSOCIAL2017

# lover in you!

Earn points from all your Harlequin book purchases from wherever you shop.

Turn your points into *FREE BOOKS* of your choice
OR
*EXCLUSIVE GIFTS* from your favorite authors or series.

Join for FREE today at
**www.HarlequinMyRewards.com.**

Harlequin My Rewards is a free program (no fees) without any commitments or obligations.

MYR17

# THE WORLD IS BETTER WITH

*Romance*

Harlequin has everything from contemporary, passionate and heartwarming to suspenseful and inspirational stories.

Whatever your mood, we have a romance just for you!

Connect with us to find your next great read, special offers and more.